THE TOP–SECRET
JOURNAL OF
Fiona Claire Jardin

Robin Cruise

HARCOURT BRACE & COMPANY
San Diego   New York   London
Printed in the United States of America

J
cruise

Tuesday, December 31

This is a test. <u>This is only a test.</u>

I don't know one thing about keeping a journal. I'm supposed to start writing one tomorrow. So this is a practice.

Mom and John Robert made me promise to write in this journal. Because of the Divorce and everything. I never had a journal before I met John Robert. He gave me this one for Christmas.

John Robert is a therapist. That's a fancy word for someone who gets to ask snoopy questions. I met him last summer, when Mom and Dad were fighting all the time and I started getting stomachaches. When I told John Robert I had forgotten how to laugh, he didn't say a word. I think he was scared of me.

Mostly John Robert and I play checkers. He's a lot better at snooping than he is at checkers.

There are only ~~six~~ seven things that are important to know about me:

1. I'm 10 years old.
2. I live near Wilmington, Delaware.
3. I'm half Irish (red hair!) and half French
   (I <u>love</u> éclairs!), even though I'm all American.
4. My parents got Divorced on November 3.
5. Soccer is my Best Sport. (I play for the
   Screaming Jonquils.)

6. My Best Friend's name is Blanca Hidalgo.
7. My Best Heroes are Emily Dickinson,
   Mother Teresa, Jewel, and Shaquille O'Neal.

Sincerely,

Fiona Claire Jardin

P.S. This journal is <u>dumb.</u>

Wednesday, January 1

So far the new year is not so great.

Sam's under his bed again. He says he's not coming out until Dad brings over his new baseball mitt. Sam will have a long wait because Dad's away on assignment for the newspaper. (He writes features for the <u>Philadelphia Inquirer.</u> He's won lots of awards.) He's doing a story about some famous brain surgeon in Cleveland. Sam is such an idiot. There's a foot of snow on the ground. What does he want his mitt for? Sam says he doesn't care about the snow. He just wants his mitt <u>and</u> he wants Dad to come home right now.

Me, too. Dad always wears goofy hats and makes lots of noise when he cooks black-eyed peas on New Year's. Black-eyed peas taste like dirt, but Dad says they're good luck. I'm crossing my fingers and toes for some good luck this year. Last year really stunk, because of my parents getting Divorced.

Is spaghetti bad luck? That's what Mom's making. She said

we could stay up until midnight last night, but she fell asleep before the big fight in <u>West Side Story.</u> Sam spilled the sparkling cider, and guess who got to clean up? I was the only one still awake to watch all the dopey people on TV when the big ball dropped at Times Square. I bet Sam will come out from under his bed soon. He loves spaghetti.

Even though John Robert gave me this journal, it was probably Mom's idea. Just because she likes to write stuff down in a journal doesn't mean I want to keep one, too. But I made a deal with them: If I write in it for 20 minutes at least three days a week, I only have to talk to John Robert at his office once a month instead of every other week. It's not that I don't like him, but I have lots more important stuff to do. Like skating on the pond with Blanca or talking on the phone with Katie. Besides, I can check in with John Robert by phone whenever I want to.

Sam's stirring the spaghetti sauce for Mom. She's pretty smart sometimes.

OK. Bye.

Friday, January 3

Dad took us out for pizza again tonight.

I never thought I'd get sick of pizza, but I am. That's what we have for dinner <u>every</u> Friday night at Dad's. (Mom makes tuna casserole every Monday night. I'm tired of tuna, too.)

We stopped at the pet store on the way home. Sam talked Dad into buying two rats! They're both males and so cute. Mostly black, with little white masks and bellies. We named them Melville and Emerson. (Don't ask about the names. My dad's crazy about American writers. He read in one of his magazines that it's good to use literary names around kids.)

We called Mom when we got back to Dad's townhouse. She tried to sound excited, but I don't think she's wild for rats. She'd like Melville and Emerson, though. They're special. At least now they can keep me and Sam company until Snippers comes home. If she ever does. That reminds me—I'd better check in with Mark at the Humane Society. He hasn't called in a couple of weeks. Mark knows everything about Snippers. He's still helping us look for her, even though she's been gone for more than a month.

Dad says Melville and Emerson can't sleep in our beds. But Sam's under his covers, and he's got Melville and a flashlight in there. Sam or Melville is making squeaky noises. Emerson's scurrying around on the little wheel in his cage. He's squeaking, too.

P.S. Mom says you don't have to sign off in your journal like you do when you write a letter. So I won't.

Monday, January 6

This journal is so stupid—it stinks.

Writing in a journal doesn't make me feel one bit better. We had to go back to school today, and my stomach hurt so bad before lunch that Miss Grimes sent me to the nurse's office to lie down for a few minutes. Miss Grimes brought me some ginger ale, but it didn't help much.

Nothing helps. It's been ~~63~~ 64 days since the Divorce. Mom says we have to move forward and that every day things will get a little easier. Nothing is one bit easier. Dad says Sam and I have to be tough. Maybe I'd be tougher if my stomach didn't hurt half the time.

At night I hear spooky things. I'm afraid to fall asleep because sometimes when I wake up I can't remember where I am. Late at night I think about Hurricane Jacqueline, when everything got turned upside down. The patio chairs flew right past my window. And the screen doors rattled like someone was trying to get in. Snippers ran in circles around the kitchen, barking like crazy.

Then it got really still and creepy, just before everything tore loose again. My dad said that calm part was the "eye" of the storm. Isn't that strange? It makes me think of this big eye hanging over everything. But that's what they call it. And that's sort of how it feels now, kind of weird and quiet.

Like I'm waiting for the storm to end.

Nurse Katz said I didn't have a fever, so she sent me back to class. Blanca traded me her Twinkies for my yogurt at lunch. Then I felt a little better!

Thursday, January 9

Miss Grimes should get a life.

She asked me if something was wrong today. Then she said I stare out the window too much. We were supposed to be talking about the bubonic plague, but thinking about the Black Death during the Middle Ages gives me goose bumps. The Plague was even worse than AIDS. Germs from rats made everybody sick, and almost half of all the people who lived in Europe died.

Ever since my mom told her about the Divorce, Miss Grimes watches me all the time. I bet she squealed to all the other teachers, too. One day she told me that lots of other kids at school have Divorced parents. She said maybe we should start a club. Duh—like that's supposed to make me feel better. Almost every day Miss Grimes asks if I want to stay after school to talk. The answer is N-O. Why is she always sticking her big nose in my business?

From my desk at school I can see across to the park. There's a huge squirrel nest in one of the trees. It must be nice to be a squirrel and just play around all day when you're not stealing scraps from kids' lunches. Squirrels don't have to worry about which nest they're supposed to go to.

Sometimes it's nice just to look out the window and drift for a while. I wonder if those squirrels know Snippers. I wish they would tell her to come home.

Monday, January 13

I'm looking at this picture I borrowed from one of Mom's photo albums.

Well, I guess I didn't exactly <u>borrow</u> it, because I put it in a pretty frame and keep it on my desk all the time. Mom said I could have the photo. She never looks at old pictures, especially if Dad's in them. Mom likes to dream about the future. She loves science fiction, and she always wonders what will happen next. Dad's a history nut. He says it's important to remember where you've been.

This picture reminds me of where I used to be, even if I'm not too sure where I'm going. (Mostly I just like to know where I <u>am</u>.) Still, I'm going to write down just what it looks like in case the picture fades away. Dad says that can happen.

That's me when I was six and lost my two front teeth. Don't I look dorky? The Tooth Fairy brought me a dollar for each tooth, and I went right out and bought a bunch of Gummi Bears. That was when I still believed in the Tooth Fairy—and before I had to wear a retainer to fix my teeth. It was Easter, and all of Mom's daffodils were in bloom. Sam stuck some jelly beans up his nose after Aunt Shaun took this picture. Mom freaked and said it was dangerous for Sam to stick jelly beans up his nose. He was in Time-Out for a <u>long</u> time that day. That's one thing about Sam—he'll try almost anything. Not me. I like to research things before I try them.

That's my mom in the denim skirt. She was a painter and had long hair then. Red, like mine. That's why Dad used to call her Red—Red Ryan. Mom doesn't paint much anymore. She had to get a job because of the Divorce. She said she wanted to go back to work anyway, since Sam and I are both in school now. But she used to like to paint a lot, and bake gingersnaps.

Mom draws buildings and houses for her friend Michael. He's an architect. Mom says she's too busy now to fuss with long hair. She also says that long hair isn't <u>professional.</u> Who cares about professional? I miss how her long hair smelled soapy and clean, and the way I could hide in it. For sure Mom laughed more when she had long hair. Maybe if I grow my hair longer, I'll remember how to laugh. Every time I start to laugh, croaky sounds come out instead.

That's my dad in the droopy sweats. He's a writer and sort of famous. (He's worked for the same newspaper since before I was born.) Some days Dad can do his work at home, on his computer. But most mornings Dad rides his bike to the station and takes the train up to Philadelphia. I love it when he takes me with him to the newsroom. It's always nuts in there. Dad says newspaper reporters have lots of energy.

My dad is really tall. I used to tell everyone that he's a giant. Maybe he's a little shorter now than he was in this picture. He's definitely chubbier, but he does a lot of sit-ups. Every day. He worries that his hair is falling out, but I don't think it is.

My dad's so handsome, he should be a movie star.

Tuesday, January 14

I fell asleep last night before I finished writing about this picture.

That was our house. Mom won't drive by it anymore because I cry every time I see those new kids' bikes out front. I can't help it. WHY DID THEY PAINT THE FRONT DOOR RED? It was solid oak. That's Snippers on the porch. I could tell she was really mad when we had to sell our house. Mom and Dad say she didn't run away because of the Divorce, but I don't know. Maybe she went looking for Dad one night and couldn't find her way back to Mom's house. Sam tried that just after we moved, and Mom had to carry him piggyback all the way home from the bus stop. Mom and Sam were crying so hard, and then we all had cocoa.

Sam wants a puppy, a girl golden retriever, just like Snippers. Mom says not now. (That usually means never.) Maybe she still prays, like I do, that Snippers will come home. I bet Mom doesn't know I can hear her calling Snippers after she tucks me and Sam into bed some nights. She still has Snippers's dish under her and Dad's big bed.

I hope this photograph never fades away. I liked that clunky old porch swing. It used to hum a little when I'd swing in it at night watching for fireflies. I had my own room in our old house. Sam did, too. We had a secret fort in those lilac bushes when the bees weren't buzzing all around. We also had a swing set, and a sandbox in the side yard. On summer days, if Mom wasn't painting in her studio out back, she'd bring us lemonade and cucumber sandwiches cut up in little triangles without the crusts.

But that big old house wasn't always fun. When Mom and Dad closed the door to the den, their voices thundered up to my room. I'd sing real loud and pull the covers over my head until I fell asleep. Usually when I woke up in the morning, it was very quiet and my dad had already gone to work. Mom would bang the pots and pans when I said I didn't want breakfast because my stomach hurt.

Sometimes I felt scared in that house, but I wasn't sure why. Maybe I knew that something bad was going to happen. Even though I didn't know much about Divorce back then. I practiced the piano and made my bed. Blanca came over almost every day, and we tried to teach Snippers to fetch, but she never would. (Mom said Snippers was too smart to fetch. Dad said Snippers was too dumb to do it right.) And I stood on my head and turned cartwheels to make my mom and dad laugh. They smiled at me, but they stopped smiling at each other.

I try to figure it out, but I still don't know for sure why my parents got Divorced. Once I asked Mom about it, and she said that she and Dad aren't the same people they were when they got married. Who are they, then?

Mom says I'm too young to understand about their problems. Dad says the same thing. My parents are so strange.

Wednesday, January 15

I went to see John Robert today.

His office is so cool. He has about a hundred windup toys. I like to try to get all of them going at once. The jumping taco is my favorite. But John Robert is a darn snoop, even if he is nice. Every time I ask him a question, he twists it back into a question about me. Plus, he doesn't really stay "on task," as Miss Grimes would say.

This is what it's like to talk with John Robert:

<u>Me</u>: "I practice all the time, but I just can't get that figure eight right. The pond's pretty bumpy, and I keep catching the toe of my left skate on the ice."

J. R.: "Fio, you said your stomach has been bothering you again. What's that about?"

<u>Me</u>: "I never get stomachaches when I'm skating."

J. R.: "Why is that?"

<u>Me</u>: "I don't know. I guess because I've been skating for a long time and I know how to do it."

J. R.: "What <u>don't</u> you know how to do, Fio?"

Me: "I don't know. Decimals?"

J. R.: "Fio, this isn't a test. There are no right or wrong answers. Do decimals make your stomach hurt?"

Me: "No."

J. R.: "Well, then, think a minute—what does?"

Me: "Being scared, I guess."

J. R.: "So what scares you?"

Me: "Hurricanes?"

J. R.: "Have you ever been in a hurricane?"

Me: "Sure. Lots of times."

J. R.: "When?"

Me: "Well, Hurricane Jacqueline."

J. R.: "Ah yes. I remember Jacqueline. What was it like for you?"

Me: "Just dark and scary."

J. R.: "Why was it scary?"

Me: "Well, the patio chairs flew by my window and Snippers barked the whole night. My mom and dad couldn't do anything to quiet her down."

J. R.: "Fio, why was that scary?"

Right. Like John Robert doesn't know the answer: That's what parents are for—to calm pets down when they get scared.

Dad's mad because I was on the phone with Blanca for 20 minutes after dinner. (I'm supposed to have a 5-minute limit on the phone, unless I'm discussing homework.) Blanca always wants to know everything John Robert and I talk about. She thinks that talking to a therapist would be interesting—she even asked if she could come with me to talk to John Robert. I don't know about that. Mostly, talking with him is pretty boring.

Maybe Blanca should be a therapist someday!

Friday, January 17

I hate this. I'm sick of going back and forth all the time.

What if I lose the key to Mom's house or to Dad's house—or to both of their houses? Then where will Sam and I go?

Sam and I are spending the night at Mom's house because Dad's in Boston and won't be home until tomorrow morning. I'm supposed to be in here packing for tomorrow, but I can't find my binoculars. Mom said I must have left them at Dad's. I know I didn't. Sam and I used the binoculars this afternoon. We were spying on the nosy old Cramptons, across the street.

Sam and I wanted to take the binoculars over to Dad's townhouse. There's nothing to do there. There are only five other kids around, and they're all older than me and Sam. Everyone acts like Sam and I have poison ivy. Dad bought us a tape so we can learn Spanish after school. He has the same tape in his car. He thinks it would be fun for me and Sam and him to learn a new language together. Then we can all speak Spanish with Blanca and her family. Has Dad ever heard of loco?

Everything's always disappearing between Mom's house and

Dad's townhouse. I'm tired of taking all my stuff back and forth. And I'm sick of sharing my room with Sam. We've been reading about puberty in P.E./Health Class, and it could happen to me. What if I get a bra someday? I'll have to undress in the closet so Sam doesn't see.

Last week my tambourine disappeared. Mom didn't even care. She just said: "Don't worry, it'll turn up sooner or later." She <u>always</u> says stupid stuff like that. Next week my backpack will be gone, then this journal. After that . . . who knows? Mom will vanish in the night, or Dad won't come back from some dumb assignment. They'll just disappear—<u>poof!</u> David's parents got divorced, and his dad moved to Tulsa. David hardly ever sees his father anymore. Liza's mom ditched them and joined a country-rock band in Alabama. It happens. If Mom or Dad moves away, what will happen to me and Sam?

It's so busy switching houses, and the rules change all the time. Mom won't let us drink soda. Dad says we can't jump on the beds. Or maybe it's the other way around. Either way, it seems like Sam and I always get in trouble for breaking the rules. How am I supposed to know what day of the week it is? Or who has my lunch box? <u>I'm only 10.</u>

Mom says that we all have to be more responsible for our own stuff, but my brain isn't big enough to remember everything. I get dizzy. Why don't Sam and I just get an apartment somewhere? Then Mom, Dad, and John Robert can move in and out with all their stuff. See how they like it. Mom gets mad if I forget one thing. She always crabs at me and Sam to pick up our junk, but her house is so small there's no place to put anything.

Mom is such a witch!

Tuesday, January 21

Mom is so great!

When she took us to school this morning and Sam ran over to the playground, Mom whispered for me to get back in the car. She said to duck down real low. Mom honked and waved at Sam. Then she whistled through her teeth and yelled, "Whooee! Hang on, Honey Bear. We're playing hooky today!" At first I thought she said hockey.

Yesterday we had a holiday for Martin Luther King Jr.'s birthday, so today makes four days in a row of no school for me! Mom and I came home after we dropped Sam off. We made a double batch of chocolate chip cookies (no nuts). Then we painted our toenails. I wanted to have a picnic down at the pond, but it started to sleet. So we made cucumber sandwiches without the crusts, got a bag of tortilla chips, and spread out the picnic blanket on Mom and Dad's four-poster. Total pig-out.

Dad used to make breakfast for Mom on Saturday mornings. He'd bring it to her with the newspaper and a towel wrapped around his head like a turban. Dad can be very mysterious. One time he brought her a baloney sandwich with pickles for breakfast. Dad was hoping the pickles would make Mom change her mind about having another baby, but they didn't work. Mom says that having me and Sam for kids is perfect.

I can't remember the last time Mom and I got to spend so much time by ourselves. I asked her to tell me about the day I was born, even though I've heard the story 10,000 times. She always tells it just the same, and now it's like I actually remember that June day. Just how the honeysuckle smelled, thick and sweet, when she woke up and knew it was time to go to the hospital. When she got Dad up, he put his shirt on backwards. They had a cup of tea and pretended they weren't scared, but Dad burned up six slices of toast. They had Popsicles for breakfast instead! Then they drove slowly through the rain to the hospital. The sun began to shine the second I was born! Mom always gets quiet at this part, about how Dad began to cry. And then he laughed, shook my hand while Mom held me, and said, "Welcome to the grand adventure, Fiona Claire Jardin!"

Now that I wrote down that story, I'll always remember it for sure. Maybe that's one good thing about having a journal. Mom fell asleep here on the bed, right in the middle of all the crumbs. She's snoring real softly. Like hummingbird wings. It's nice to listen to the sleet and the branches scratching the window. Mom made me promise I won't tell Sam about today. I put my hand on my heart and said, "Scout's honor." (Mom must have forgotten that I quit Scouts last year.)

Maybe I won't tell Sam, unless he makes me really mad. If

only Dad would come home now, and waltz me and Mom around the living room like he used to at our old house.

Friday, January 24

Katie called this morning to ask me over after school. She wants me to stay for dinner, too.

Dad said I should go, because Katie's my Second-Best Friend and everything. But sometimes I don't want to hang around with her. Her house is always so cozy and organized. Katie's mom teaches kindergarten. She's very peppy, and she has long blond hair pulled back in a ponytail. Mrs. Larkin gets home from work early every day and bakes cookies or brownies and other good stuff. (Katie never eats more than one cookie. She worries all the time about her weight, even though she's as skinny as a stick.) Then Katie's dad comes home and hugs and kisses everybody. Even me. Mr. Larkin is a lawyer, and he wears a blue suit to work every single day. Except on Saturdays—then he wears a blue sweater, a white shirt, and a red tie. Katie's dad calls her Poky-Pie.

The Larkins are so rich. Katie even has her own phone line. Mr. and Mrs. Larkin always hold hands and goof around. It makes me feel sick inside to watch them. My mom and dad used to hold hands, but they stopped. How come? Mom thinks Dad's a really good writer, but she didn't like him traveling so much. One summer Dad didn't have to go away on assignment for six weeks in a row, but he got kind of grouchy. He said he has to go where the good stories take him, so he started traveling a lot again. Dad thinks Mom's paintings are so great, he kept telling her to open a gallery and sell her work so she could make some money. Mom said that selling her paintings would be like selling me and Sam. For a while she quit painting and took golf lessons instead.

Mom stinks at golf. She sold her clubs to Mrs. Larkin at the garage sale we had before we moved. Mrs. Larkin is taking lessons from the pro at the club.

Monday, January 27

Today Miss Grimes told us about the idea of a billion.

A billion is the number that comes after all the hundred millions. 1,000,000,000. That's a billion. If you counted one number every second of your life, it would take you thirty years—all day every day—to count to a billion!

Thirty whole years. That's almost as old as my dad. He's 38 and Mom is 36. Dad used to say that even though he's older than Mom, she's wiser and prettier. He probably doesn't think so anymore.

I didn't realize it until a few weeks ago, but Natalie Winter lives right around the corner from Mom's house. She hardly ever says anything. Some days she smiles at me and sits next to me at lunch. Mom usually offers her a ride home from the bus stop. Natalie always says, "Not today, thank you!" Then she waves good-bye.

Natalie Winter is very polite.

Mrs. Howard is a really nice piano teacher—she smells like lilacs and her laugh sounds like a bell ringing. But no matter how much I practice, I'll never get any better.

I've been taking lessons since last summer, but I just can't get my left hand going. Mom asked me to remind Dad about the check for piano lessons when I talk to him tonight. I pretended like I didn't hear her. John Robert says that Sam and I are <u>not</u> messengers. He says that if Mom and Dad need to talk, that's their business.

Mom is always cranky about money. I don't want to play the piano anyway. It's boring and I'm no good at it. But M-O-M says I can't quit—she says I'll never get really good if I don't practice every day. Just because Wolfgang Amadeus Mozart was composing music by the time he was 5 doesn't mean it's easy for a 10-year-old kid like me to play the piano.

I'd rather just learn to play the saxophone with Dad. But Mom says it doesn't count that he and I take a lesson together every week. She says I need to work harder on my own, that music isn't a game, like Ping-Pong. I don't get it. Music is music. I can already play Beethoven's "Ode to Joy" from his Ninth Symphony on the piano. That's good enough. Sam can't even play "Three Blind Mice."

I'm sick of writing in this dumb journal. I have 10 minutes to go. Blah, blah, blah, blah, blah . . .

Thursday, January 30

This must be a dream.

Dylan came right over and sat next to me and Blanca at lunch today. He gave me half of his tuna-with-sprouts sandwich. Dylan's already 11, and he draws way better than everyone in the whole fifth grade. Maybe the whole school. Plus, he's a whiz at decimals. I'm good at math, but there's no way I can do decimals.

I like the way Dylan's hair sticks up in back. He's got a good smile, too. It makes him look all sunny. Mostly he draws spaceships and aircraft carriers. His dancing trees and dragons are amazing. He owes me 50¢ because we bet on the Super Bowl and he lost. Dylan always bets on the Patriots. No matter what. Me and my dad like Green Bay. I told Dylan that he could keep his 50¢ if he gave me his enchanted forest drawing. It's so G-R-E-A-T! He said maybe.

I saw Katie talking to Dylan during recess. I bet they were talking about how my parents are Divorced and everything. I bet that's all Katie ever talks about.

Maybe I should get a new Second-Best Friend.

MY BEST FRIEND
By Fiona Claire Jardin

Blanca Lucia Galvez Hidalgo is my Best Friend.

Blanca has been my Best Friend since we were both 3. She used to live just two houses away from me on Orchard Lane, before my parents got Divorced. Now our parents have to drive us to each other's house. But Blanca is still my Best Friend.

I like her because:

1. She always shares her brownies.
2. She has thick, shiny hair and straight teeth.
3. She has her own CD player, and she totally L-O-V-E-S Jewel.
4. She cried and hugged me tight when I told her my mom and dad were getting Divorced.
5. She still likes to play jacks—and sometimes she lets me win.
6. I hate nuts and fish sticks, and <u>she</u> hates nuts and fish sticks.
7. She plays soccer for the Screaming Jonquils just because I don't want to play soccer without her.
8. She speaks English <u>and</u> Spanish.

21

9. She is a good singer.
10. She can do back bends and walk-overs.

Sunday, February 2

My room is getting better—at Mom's <u>and</u> at Dad's.

Today me and Mom and Sam painted the room that Sam and I share at her house. It's lemon-drop yellow with robin's-egg-blue trim. When the sun shines in through the windows, it's like being in a warm, sunny nest. And Dad got me and Sam these great high beds with desks built in underneath them at his townhouse.

Sam's got one wall plastered with all the same stuff at Mom's <u>and</u> Dad's: posters of Ken Griffey Jr., R2D2, Michael Jordan, John Elway, and The Artist Formerly Known As Prince. (Don't ask about Prince—Sam saw him on MTV at Matt's house and thinks he is so cool. I think he is totally strange.)

One of the worst things about sharing a room with Sam is that his bedtime is 8:00. I stay up until 9:00, but I can't read in bed before I fall asleep because the light bugs Sam. Mom and I usually read for a while after Sam goes to bed, but sitting in the living room isn't the same as being all cuddled up in your bed.

It's horrible to share a room with your dweebie little brother. Especially if he is always curious. I put PRIVATE signs on my desk and dresser, but Sam says <u>private</u> is a big word and he can't read it. He also says he doesn't know what <u>private</u> means. Ha! Sam's a big fibber. His kindergarten teacher said he reads

22

at the second-grade level—and Dad has made him look up private in the dictionary a bunch of times.

Samuel Miles Jardin is a dope.

Wednesday, February 5

When Dad picked me and Sam up for breakfast on the way to school this morning, I could see Mom getting smaller and smaller in the rearview mirror as we drove down the street.

She looked so sad and tiny. When she waved good-bye, her hand was flopping around like a fish. I asked Dad if she could at least come to breakfast with us, but he got that worried look. (His eyes squish together and his forehead gets all wrinkly.) Then he said that maybe Mom could come with us another day. Yeah, right. Dad started to whistle "Yankee Doodle." He always tries to change the subject when Sam or I talk about Mom. She wouldn't have come with us anyway. Mom would rather go to the dentist than have breakfast with Dad.

I snuck to the principal's office at lunch and called Mom at work, but she was in a meeting. My stomach was hurting again. There was a message on the machine at Dad's when Sam and I got home from school. Mom sounded all chirpy. Why is she so happy all of a sudden?

I called Mom back, but she wasn't home. Where is she? Dad says Mom has a life, and we all need to respect her privacy. He says she can take care of herself. Dad also says that I watch too much TV news and that I should play more hopscotch. (I do like hopscotch. Chinese jump rope and dodgeball, too.) It's a good thing Dad doesn't know that Mom doesn't ever let Sam and me watch TV news, or we wouldn't know anything that's happening in the world. Sometimes it seems like a miracle that my mom and dad were married for 14 whole years.

It's bedtime, and Mom still hasn't called us back. <u>Where is she?</u> If Dad answers the phone when she calls, she'll probably hang up. I was hoping she would sing that mockingbird song to me and Sam.

I always sleep better when Mom sings that song.

Sunday, February 7

This is amazing!

Melville had eight babies! They're all pink and they have the tiniest eyes. We didn't even know Melville was pregnant. The lady at the pet store said she was a <u>guy.</u> Dad let us skip church for once because of all the ruckus, and Blanca came over for breakfast. Dad helped her and me and Sam clean out the rats' cage. We put in some cotton balls and fresh water and shredded newspaper. Now those squeaky babies are all nestled in with Melville. Sam named them after the Seven Dwarfs: Grumpy, Dopey, Sleepy, Sneezy, Bashful, Happy, and Doc. I only got to name one: Madonna. Emerson's in one of the recycling bins till Dad can get him his own cage when the pet store opens. Dad's so mad at the pet store lady.

Sam's pitching a fit. Mom's picking us up at noon, and Sam

doesn't want to go to her house. He's worried something might happen to the babies. He called Mom first thing this morning. He said that he decided to live with Emerson and Melville and their babies at Dad's. Mom said no way.

So now Sam's trying to pack up the cage, but Dad said it's not good for babies to go back and forth in the cold. <u>Duh.</u>

Wednesday, February 12

If John Robert is a real doctor, how come he always wears blue jeans and a denim shirt?

Mostly I think he's a real pain in the butt. <u>Trust and safety, safety and trust</u>—that's all John Robert ever talks about. He sounds like an old cassette that got tangled up in my tape player. He's always tugging at his beard or cleaning his glasses. He sure fidgets a lot for someone who's supposed to make you feel calm. And he's got photographs of flowers and birds on his walls. <u>Boring!</u>

John Robert gets to ask me all kinds of questions, but I barely know anything about him. He says I can ask him anything I want, but he always twists things back around to me. He spent the whole hour today asking me about crying.

> <u>J. R.</u>: "Fio, you said you never cried when your mom and dad first decided to live apart. How come?"
>
> <u>Me</u>: "I guess I'm very brave. Everybody says so."

J. R.: "What do YOU say?"
Me: "About what?"
J. R.: "About being brave."
Me: "I never cry, so I must be. Brave, I mean.
But I guess I'm not very funny—you know,
since I still can't remember how to laugh.
Could I take lessons somewhere?"
J. R.: "Maybe crying would be a good lesson,
Fio. Who knows? Crying might help you
remember how to laugh."

No way I'd fall for that trick. Once I start to cry, I'll never be able to stop.

Me (pointing to one of John Robert's dumb
photos): "Hey, isn't that a black-capped
chickadee?"

Today was Ash Wednesday and Abraham Lincoln's birthday. Dad went to church on his way home from work. He still has a black smudge on his forehead.

Friday, February 14

Happy Valentine's Day!

I got 17 valentines and Sam got 26, except he threw away all the ones from girls. He did keep the one that Lucy made, with the hopping toads all over it. Sam says Lucy doesn't really count as a girl because she has short hair and can whistle through her fingers, just like him.

Dad wrote us a poem—actually, it's a limerick. He wrote it in crayon on butcher paper and rolled it out on the kitchen table before Sam and I got up for breakfast:

> *There once was a lefty named Sam,*
> *Who was the most mischievous ham.*
> *His sister, named Fio, sang opera con brio,*
> *And both kids were the best in the land.*
>
> Happy Valentine's Day, my little quahogs!
>
> Love, Daddy-O

My dad doesn't feel like he's doing his job unless he makes me and Sam look words up in the dictionary at least once a day. He said that con brio is Italian for "with great energy and feeling." A quahog is a clam. (I looked it up.)

Mom left amazing valentines for Sam and me at Dad's front door. She must have stayed up the whole night gluing all those doilies and Cheerios together. Sam and I are idiots—we forgot to mail hers. She'll be sad not to get a valentine from us. I'm afraid to ask Dad to drive us over to her house. And now it's too late to mail them. What good is a valentine if it's two days late? I'm always messing up, even when I try to remember everything.

Dylan gave me his old notebook. It's a navy blue binder with NFL stickers all over it. It's a little grody, but I think he must like me. Why else would he give me his notebook? Katie says it's garbage, but she's not very romantic. Maybe she's jealous.

My dad is really romantic. One year he hired a violinist to come play for my mom on Valentine's Day. It was some song they knew from a long time ago in France. That's where they met. In Paris. They were both college students, and they were so poor they had candles instead of lamps. Isn't that romantic?

When my dad hired that violinist at our old house and the two of them started to dance, my mom laughed and then began to cry. She said she missed my dad so much—even though he was <u>right there,</u> dancing with her!

I can almost hear that music and see my mom and dad floating together. It makes my stomach hurt to think about that. What would it be like if Dylan and I got married someday? Maybe it would be nice. But where would my mom and dad sit at our wedding? And what if Dylan got really mad at me about something and we got a Divorce?

If we <u>do</u> get married, we'll probably go bowling afterwards. Dylan's big on bowling. I'm big on gutter balls. But I don't think I will—get married, I mean. And if I do, for sure I won't get Divorced. No matter what.

Sunday, February 16

I never really knew about Joint Custody until last year. It means that if you're a kid whose parents are Divorced, both your mom and dad take care of you. There's all kinds of legal stuff parents have to work out with the Judge when they get Divorced. Mom and Dad explained a lot of it to me and Sam. Except Sam wasn't interested, and I didn't want to talk about all that. How they were going to divide up all their stuff. What to do with the house. How they were going to take care of me and Sam. What they'd do about money.

At first my mom thought we should live with her. Because Dad travels sometimes. But my dad thought we should live with him until Mom figured out what she was going to do about a job. Finally they agreed that me and Sam should live with both of them.

We go to Mom's house three days a week (Sunday, Monday, and Tuesday) and Dad's townhouse three days a week (Wednesday, Thursday, and Friday). We take turns with them every other Saturday night. That's how they worked it out with the Judge who gave them the Divorce. He said that a lot of times kids live mostly with one parent or the other. But he said we could try it this way as long as Sam and I seem OK.

It only takes 11 minutes to drive from Mom's house to Dad's. Dad lives right in town. He can walk or bike to the train station, so he hardly ever drives up to Philadelphia. Mom lives at the very edge of town. She likes being near the pond and surrounded by trees. Besides, she needs a big yard so she can garden.

I guess that's one good thing about living in a small town—at least my parents still live close to each other. Dad says that when Sam and I are a little older, we can ride our bikes back and forth. Mom says we'll see about that.

Wednesday, February 19

My parents are liars and cheats.

Sam and I aren't going to Dad's this afternoon. Mom said Dad called early this morning because he has to stay an extra day for some story he's researching in Boston. Mom's making pancakes for breakfast—like that will cheer us up. Right.

Dad hasn't even called back to talk to me and Sam. And he didn't leave a number so we could call him. I hate it when they trick us like that. Sam said we should call the President and report Dad. Dad promised us he'd come home early today so we could throw the football around at the park before dinner. There's no way Mom will play with us. She'll probably make us clean out all the closets or clip our toenails.

Mom didn't care one bit that Dad broke his promise. She just said she was sorry that I was so mad, but stuff like that happens. She sounds like a zombie when she talks like that—all flat and quiet: "You need to discuss this matter with Your Father, Fiona Claire. I'm sorry you feel so disappointed, but Your Father and I are trying hard to do a better job of planning our time with you and Sam." How come she always calls Dad "Your Father"? She used to call him Marty. Or Mr. X if he was in trouble. (Dad's first name is Xavier, but no one ever calls him that except Mama Jardin.)

I bet Dad didn't even want to come home early. He'd rather fool around on his computer than play with us. I bet he met some lady and decided to stay over in Boston. Ladies are always calling him and giggling and leaving dumb messages on the answering machine. Maybe they should get a life. Dad probably didn't even remember to call Simon to cancel our saxophone lesson tonight. Too bad for Dad—he'll have to pay for it anyway.

Mom's crabbing at me. I'd better hurry or we'll be late for school.

Saturday, February 22

I <u>might</u> change my favorite color from purple to turquoise.

I still like purple, but that's Katie's favorite color. And Maggie's. Purple isn't very original. Besides, eggplant is purple. So are bruises. And pickled beets. <u>Yuck!</u>

The thing is, purple has been my favorite color for three whole years. And now I've got lots of purple stuff. My bike is purple. Barrettes. Shoelaces. Sweats. Socks. Even the plastic mouthpiece of my retainer has a purple stripe. Turquoise would be like starting all over again. And if turquoise is my favorite color, Dawn will think I'm copying her because turquoise has been <u>her</u> favorite since she was 6!

Chartreuse is good, but I'm not sure I'm a chartreuse kind of girl. Maybe I should just keep purple. I'll call Blanca. She always knows what to do. Except she likes everything white, and that's not even a color. White is the absence of all color. (Miss

Weller spent two whole art classes blabbing about black and white—like we didn't already know that smushing all colors together makes black and not having any colors at all makes white.)

The moon is full tonight. And the sky is <u>so</u> clear. Today is George Washington's official birthday. Everyone knows he was the first president. But until Miss Grimes told us yesterday, I didn't know he had <u>nine</u> brothers and sisters. Or that his dad died when George was just 11. I'll be 11 on June 1.

How could any 11-year-old kid's dad die? My dad is very sturdy. He's 38. Papa Jardin is nowhere near dead, and he's almost 70! Grandpappy Ryan died four years ago, but he was 79. Plus, he had smoked ever since he was 14. (I'll be dead, too, if I ever smoke—because my mom and dad will kill me for sure.)

I'm glad Mom made Dad promise to quit smoking before they got married. Every once in a while he smokes a cigar and really stinks up everything.

Tuesday, February 25

Sam's still on the phone with Dad.

They've been talking for 20 minutes, and Sam won't hang up. He said that Mom doesn't do the voices right when she reads to us at night. From now on he wants Dad to read the bedtime story even when we're at Mom's house. Sam said Mom should buy a speaker phone for our room.

Mom says there's no right or wrong way to read a book out loud. It's just that her way and Dad's way are different. She's always saying stupid stuff like that. Sam says that Mom should be more like Dad. He tells Dad the same thing about Mom. Mom also says that she'll buy a singing pig before she buys a speaker phone.

Dad sounded so far away and snuffly tonight. He would never say that he gets sad or lonely, but sometimes maybe he does. When I asked what he was doing, he said he was just hanging out with J. S. B., and cleaning out Melville's and Emerson's cages. My dad always says Johann Sebastian Bach is his best friend. (My mom feels sort of like that about some geezer named Roy Orbison.) He promised to be careful about the babies, but he said we have to find them new homes pretty soon. No way. <u>They're ours.</u> At least I should get to keep Madonna. That would make it three boys (counting Emerson) and three girls (counting Melville and Madonna) around there.

Then Dad said, "G'night, mugwump," and he told me to put Sam back on the phone. When I asked him, "What's a <u>mugwump?</u>" he told me to look it up. He always tells me that!

I wish Dad lived across the street instead of the creepy Cramptons. I'd make him cocoa with marshmallows to cheer him up. I hope Dad's OK.

Tuesday, March 4

It doesn't matter how much I write in this journal—<u>nothing ever changes.</u>

Mom is grumpy about money and worries about work all the

time. What if she messes up and Michael fires her? She keeps adding and subtracting bunches of numbers, but she can't ever make them come out right. Even when we play Scrabble, it's like she's somewhere else—on Mars. Or Jupiter. Dad always forgets stuff and makes promises he doesn't keep. Sam acts like a baby and messes with my stuff, and he <u>never</u> gets in trouble. My mom says she counts on me. She says that Sam is still having a hard time because he's only 5, so he needs lots of help and special attention. I say he's just a selfish brat.

When you're 10 you're supposed to be brave and strong, even if you don't feel that way. But no one except John Robert asks me how I feel or what I want. If they did, I would tell them: I'm sad. I'm mad at my parents for messing up my life. My stomach hurts. All day every day, I feel like I want to go home. But I'm not sure where that is. I feel lost. And alone.

Mostly I feel really, really scared. I want my mother. I want my father. I even want Sam. And Snippers. But I want us all together. Just like we used to be. In our big old house on Orchard Lane. I want to wake up from this bad dream and have breakfast with my family: granola with raisins and sliced banana, buttermilk waffles with real maple syrup, and peach smoothies.

I can write in this journal every day, but nothing is going to change. Ever.

Natalie Winter and I walked home from the bus stop today.

She told me a dirty joke—about a pig that rolled in the mud! Natalie is really nice.

I'm going to call Blanca and tell her the "dirty" joke.

Thursday, March 6

Toes are so strange if you think about them.

What good are toes? And why are there five of them on each foot—why not four? Or seven? Why are they on the front of your feet instead of the back? Or the sides? It would be more interesting if toes were stuck to your heels. Except maybe then you wouldn't know which way to go.

Why aren't toes more like fingers? At least monkey toes are good for something. Like swinging around in the trees. Dad wrote a story about some kid who was born without any arms. That kid did <u>everything</u> with his feet. He even buttoned his shirt with his toes. I just tried that. <u>No way.</u>

My toes look like chubby jelly beans. I definitely got my dad's feet—all flat and smashed. And as big as boats. I wear size 6½ in ladies' shoes, and I'm only in fifth grade. Mom says that probably means I'll be tall, like Dad. But it probably just means I'll end up with his big stinky feet.

Sam's toes are way better than mine. They're long and bendy. Maybe if Sam starts practicing now, he could play the piano with his feet and make us lots of money. I could be his manager.

Sunday, March 9

Sam and I are staying with Dad all week!

Mom had to meet with some client of Michael's who lives near Granny Ryan, so she decided to spend the whole week in Philadelphia, instead of going back and forth. I'm sort of glad Granny's not coming down here again. She always follows me and Sam around. She touches our foreheads, and she asks what we're thinking about and if we're taking our vitamins. Her hands are all cold and bony. And you can see the veins, like squiggly worms, right through her skin.

Last time she was here, Granny told Mom that when she married Pappy Ryan it was for good—and what's the matter with husbands and wives these days? (Granny said that being married to Pappy for 57 years was no picnic, but they made a promise to each other in front of God and everybody.) Granny said there's a Divorce epidemic and that doctors should give everyone a "patience" shot and make them take a hard test before they get married. Mom just kept washing the dishes and humming real loud.

Softball practice starts tomorrow. Katie and I are on the same team again this season: the East Side Cardinals. Darn! I <u>hate</u> red. (Katie says red isn't such a great color on me, on account of my hair and freckles.) I wish I could have been on the Tanagers or even the Orioles instead.

Blanca is so lucky. She's on the Flamingos. They have really cool Day-Glo pink shirts, socks, and hats, with black shorts. I don't care what Dad says. I am <u>not</u> pitching this year, even if he is the assistant coach. Sometimes I wish he would just keep his big mouth shut.

Katie says that playing left field is great. She hardly ever has to make a play.

Wednesday, March 12

Every time I see John Robert, I keep thinking there's something I'm supposed to know. He always listens really hard to everything I say, and then he nods or puts his hands together like he's praying. Sometimes I feel like I'm taking a pop quiz when I talk to him—and I can't understand even one of the questions.

I thought that maybe the thing I'm supposed to know has something to do with Dad. When Dad moved out of our old house and started looking for a place to live, I was afraid that Sam and I wouldn't see him as much. He's sort of forgetful. And he's always thinking about whatever story he's working on. I thought maybe Dad would get a different job and move away. Like David's dad did after he and Mrs. Jordan got Divorced. And I worried that Dad wouldn't know what to do without Mom to organize everything.

I don't worry about any of that too much anymore. When Mom and Dad got Joint Custody, they had to figure out everything. John Robert said that's their job, because they're the parents. I told John Robert that I bet Dad's going to be OK.

Sometimes it seems like Dad actually spends more time than he used to with me and Sam instead of less. And he always knows everything that's going on with us. John Robert nodded but didn't say much.

> J. R.: "Fio, why are you worrying about your father?"
>
> Me: "Well, because he's my dad."
>
> J. R.: "So you're supposed to worry about him because you're his daughter?"
>
> Me: "No, but my mom doesn't watch out for him anymore."
>
> J. R.: "Is there some reason your dad needs someone to watch out for him?"
>
> Me: "Not really. I mean, he's a grown-up and everything. But . . ."
>
> J. R.: "But what, Fio?"

I guess Dad and Mom are supposed to watch out for themselves. John Robert and I haven't played checkers in months. Maybe he got tired of losing all the time.

Monday, March 17

Mom gets home tonight!

It sure doesn't seem like Saint Patrick's Day without her, even though Dad made green pancakes. They looked more like oozing brains than shamrocks.

Maybe Sam will come out from under his bed. He's mad because we had to take Melville's babies to the pet store yesterday. Even Madonna. Blanca renamed Dopey—she calls him Elvis—and took him to her house on Saturday, but Mrs. Hidalgo made Blanca give Dopey-Elvis right back to Dad.

Dad said the babies are getting too big for us to keep them. He said the pet store will find them nice homes. Sam said something really mean about how he'll never send his babies away from him even for one day. He's been under his bed since before lunch. What if he has to go to the bathroom? Sometimes I'm afraid Sam will explode, he gets so mad. He screams and cries and slams the door all the time. I told John Robert that Sam's out of control. John Robert doesn't care one bit.

The worst part about staying with Dad all week is Mrs. Dudley. Sam calls her Mrs. Deadly. She picks us up from school on Wednesdays, Thursdays, and Fridays. She starts dinner if Dad isn't home by 5:30 or so. Mom gets off at 2:30 on Mondays and Tuesdays, so we don't have a sitter at her house. She's usually there to meet the bus when Sam and I get off. (Sam has to stay for extended day every afternoon, but he likes it.) Mom or Dad drives us to school in the morning on the way to work. I'm glad I don't have to take the stinky old bus both ways.

Dad says Mrs. Dudley is sweet. (P.U.! I think she smells like boiled cabbage.) He also says that just because Mom's gone doesn't mean he can take the whole week off from work. Mrs. Dudley doesn't pick <u>him</u> up at work wearing shoes that look like milk cartons and her eyes going in different directions.

Sam wouldn't get in Mrs. D.'s ratty old car after school today. She chased him halfway down the block. She's pretty fast, even with those dorky shoes.

Dad is going to take us over to Mom's after dinner. I wonder what she'll bring me from her trip. I hope Granny Ryan doesn't send me another sweater, size XL. She always says I'll grow into whatever it is she buys me. How come grown-ups always say you'll get bigger instead of seeing you the way you are? Who wants to go around looking like something out of the Macy's Thanksgiving Day Parade?

Thursday, March 20

No wonder I hate decimals.

This is the dumbest word problem: "Mr. and Mrs. Miller are shopping for a new color television set. They found one on sale for $385, including a remote control. The salesperson said the Millers would get an additional 5% discount if they pay cash for the television. He said they could also put $85 down on the TV and pay off the rest at 8% interest in 12 easy installments. How much will the Millers pay for the TV set if they pay cash? If they choose the installment plan?"

There are too many things going on in this problem, and Dad refuses to help me with it. He says I can figure out the answer, step by step. I say the Millers probably don't even need another color TV. Don't they know that Americans watch too much television? Maybe they should just donate some money to save the rainforest instead. Mom doesn't approve of buying anything unless you can pay cash. (She doesn't believe in credit and installment plans.) Dad thinks it's foolish not to take advantage of credit at no extra cost. And what does the remote control have to do with anything?

I twisted my ankle at softball practice. Dad told me to slide into third base, but I didn't do it right. He taped my ankle up really good afterwards. Katie refuses to slide. Ever.

Only one more day till spring break!

Tuesday, March 25

Katie stopped by this morning to see if I wanted to ride bikes.

We're off all week. So is Katie's mom, and her dad took the day off, too. It's sunny and warm for a change. Mr. and Mrs. Larkin were riding that dumb tandem bicycle of theirs—sometimes they look more like kids than parents. I told Katie I couldn't go with them because I was working on my book report.

Actually, I finished my book report last weekend. (I read The Secret Garden again. Miss Grimes doesn't know that I read it last year, too. This time I read the whole book—311 pages—in one week. It took me a month to read it last year. I'm glad I'm not an orphan, even though Mary Lennox had a lot of adventures once she moved from India to her uncle's house in England. Sam and Dad should call me Mem Sahib because I'm the lady of Dad's house.)

I just didn't want to ride bikes with the smoochy Larkins. Even though they had packed a picnic and were going for ice cream afterwards. Katie says I'm lucky because I've got Sam. Yeah, right. Katie's lucky because her mom buys <u>all</u> of her clothes at the Gap. Sometimes I wish something bad would happen to Katie—like her hair would turn green or Miss Grimes would send her to the principal's office. Nothing ever does, though. No matter what, her hair is always smooth and blond. And Miss Grimes never yells at her. Katie will never ever get sent to the principal's office.

Sunday, March 30

It's Easter <u>and</u> it's Dad's birthday!

That doesn't usually happen, but this year it did. Sam and I made him frozen waffles with ice cream and chocolate syrup for breakfast. We got him a game of chess for his computer. Mom helped us pay for it (mostly, she paid), but Sam and I made the card.

We left a big mess at Dad's because we had to hurry up and get ready for church. Those choir ladies pinched me on the cheek after the service and said, "Oh my! Haven't you grown?!" Somehow both of the new dresses Dad bought me had ended up at Mom's house. So the dress I wore to church was a girl's size 8, even though I'm usually a 12—and I'm not one bit fat. (Katie likes to remind me that I weigh 7 pounds more than she does. I remind her that I'm 2¼ inches taller.)

I don't see why we have to go to church all the time. Especially on Dad's birthday. But he always takes us when we're with him, then drops us off at Mom's afterwards. Church is so boring, except the part about Jesus rising from the dead. That's interesting and mysterious. (Miracles are cool.) Mom never goes to church, so why should we? She says that God is everywhere and church is where you make it. (Granny Ryan would have a cow if she heard Mom say that. Granny goes to Mass every single morning.) Dad says that going to church is one way to be sure we make time for God. He also says that we can decide what to do about religion when we're Mom's age. Until then Sam and I have to go to church with him.

I can't wait that long to decide. I'll die of boredom in a few more years. John Robert says moms and dads shouldn't confuse their kids by telling them different things and disagreeing about important stuff like religion. Maybe I should remind Mom and Dad.

We hunted for Easter eggs in the courtyard at church. I found 13. I hope that's not bad luck. Some lady named Sarah laughed and put her hand on Dad's shoulder. It was like slow motion. She sounded like a horse and her lips were really dark purple.

At least Sam didn't put jelly beans up his nose. Dad gave me a stuffed lop-eared bunny. I told him it's dumb for an almost-11-year-old girl to get a stuffed animal, but I named her Rosalind and tucked her in my bed. I'm glad Dad got me Rosalind. She's very soft and cuddly.

Mom had an egg hunt for us at her house, too. The Hidalgos came over for dinner. Blanca's little sister, Francesca, brought her new baby chick. She named him Ralph! And Mrs. Hidalgo sang some songs in Spanish. We had leg of lamb, roasted vegetables, and coconut cake shaped like a bunny. (No way I'd eat a lamb. Mom still forgets every once in a while that I'm a vegetarian. I'm not <u>strictly</u> vegetarian, though—I do eat dairy products and fish, chicken, and turkey. She wasn't happy when I made myself a cucumber-and-cream-cheese sandwich, but she didn't make a fuss.) The cake was fantastic. Blanca's dad had three pieces. No wonder he's chubby and jolly!

Dad said today was his last birthday. That's because next year he'll be 40—so from now on he's going to stay <u>39!</u>

Sam and I have to go back to school tomorrow.

Tuesday, April 1

<u>Laurel Rose Ryan + X. Martin Jardin.</u>

My mom and dad came to pick me and Sam up early from school today. They brought Snippers and Melville and Emerson and all the babies. And a huge picnic basket filled with caramel corn and root beer. They had white and silver balloons tied all over the car, and streamers everywhere. Someone had sprayed JUST MARRIED—AGAIN!!! on the back window.

Mom was wearing this long, shimmery lavender skirt with tiny silver stars speckled all over it. She had white rosebuds in her hair. Dad's hair was slicked back, and he smelled like limes.

He was wearing his leather jacket and sunglasses. Both of them were laughing. They looked like movie stars.

When Mom and Dad saw me and Sam, they swooped us up in their arms. We all danced and laughed and cried. And then Dad said: "Surprise, surprise, our sweet little quahogs!"

April Fool!

Monday, April 7

Some weirdo called the wrong number today just before dinner.

Mom was out back, poking around in the garden. The guy asked for "Laurie." Laurie? I told him there's no Laurie here. There's a Laurel Ryan Jardin. But definitely no <u>Laurie.</u> He got all quiet, and then he said, "Uh, OK. You must be Fiona. Could you please just tell your mom that Howard called?"

How did he know my name? Maybe I should call the police. He was very polite and he did say <u>please,</u> but I told him that he had the wrong number. Then I hung up fast. <u>Howard?</u> Get real. My mom doesn't know anyone named Howard. Even if she did, she'd never call him back. My mom has me and Sam. She doesn't have time to talk to guys on the phone—or to go to the movies or bowling. Besides, Mom doesn't want to get married again. And she'll never ever find anyone half as good as Dad.

I forgot to tell Mom about that wrong number. Tomorrow is Blanca's birthday! My dad and I got her a geode for her collection—and my mom got her rhinestone barrettes like mine.

Wednesday, April 9

John Robert didn't care one bit that Mom bought some new paints and canvas.

I told him that my mom quit painting a long time ago. And that she's really good at it. Her quitting painting is like my quitting soccer. Or quitting as Blanca's Best Friend. Or like Sam quitting T-ball. You don't just quit doing the things you really love, right?

Mom bought paints, so she must be thinking about making a painting. My mom used to be happy all the time when she painted. Sam and I could hear her singing in the studio out back. Sometimes she forgot what time it was, and we had to remind her to make lunch. But we didn't care, because she was always right there with us.

John Robert didn't say a word when I said maybe my mom is going to be OK. He just fiddled with his glasses. He asked me for the 100th time if I ever felt like crying because of the Divorce.

It's staying light out later since daylight savings time started on Sunday. It was barely dark when Dad and I got home from our saxophone lesson.

Thursday, April 10

I like Dad's study.

It smells like Dad in here—pine and limes. He's got books and magazines stacked all around. Mom always used to say

Dad's study was a rat nest, but that's how we like it. Not Mom. She likes to be organized.

One whole wall of Dad's study is covered with pictures of all the Jardins: There's Papa Jardin tossing horseshoes, and Mama Jardin on the glider. Aunt Louise and Uncle Fred. Aunt Judythe and Uncle Ray. Uncle Phillip and Aunt Susan. Uncle Maxwell and Aunt Lisa. And Uncle Harvey. And bunches of cousins: Nancy and Meghan, Matthew and Glen. Alex and Jessica, Whitney and Alison. Lillian and Beatrice. Matt, Spencer, and Karl. Dad took down all the pictures of Mom and put them in a box somewhere. But I can see her way at the back of everybody in a photograph he took up at Mama and Papa Jardin's cottage on the Fourth of July the summer before they got married. Mom looks like a college girl. I guess Dad missed that one. How can you be married to someone for 14 years and then put all of her pictures in a box?

I can find out all kinds of things in Dad's study—about King Tut and space shuttles, Emily Dickinson and fruit bats. His computer plays a little Bach prelude whenever you turn it on. And this is where I keep my snow globes. I have 37 of them. (I'm trying to get 100, for each of the 50 states and for 50 foreign cities.) If I shake real fast, I can get the snow going in every one. So it's snowing on Mount Rushmore and the Vatican and Disneyland at the very same time!

All the snow has stopped falling now, except for in my Lake Placid globe. It's my favorite, even though I wasn't even born when Granny and Pappy Ryan took Mom and Aunt Shaun and

Uncle Will and Aunt Kathleen to the Winter Olympics on Lake Placid a long, long time ago. The sky is inky blue, with a full yellow moon. And there's a girl in a red skating skirt with gold trim doing a spin on the ice all by herself. The snow is falling around her so lightly. Like feathers. I learned how to ice-skate when I was 3, but I'll never get that spin right.

I wonder what we'll do about Christmas this year. Maybe it won't come. I like all the cookies, and decorating the house and caroling. And the presents! But last Christmas was all gray and blurry. Mom didn't want anyone to visit except Granny Ryan. It was so quiet without all the Jardins and the Ryans singing and gabbing. Dad went to the shore to spend Christmas Eve with Mama and Papa Jardin last year. Sam and I waited forever for him to come get us on Christmas Day, but when he did, Mom didn't even ask him in for mulled cider. Dad drove us over to his house, and we made cocoa and watched the sky for shooting stars.

Christmas didn't seem like magic at all last year.

Tuesday, April 15

That does it.

I'm never going to sleep again at Mom's stupid house. It's creepy, there are weird noises, and now I have to stay awake every minute if I want to catch the crook. That dumb thief had better watch out—and I mean it.

My roller skates are gone! They vanished. Mom says I probably left my skates at Dad's. But I know I didn't leave them over there. Did my skates <u>fly</u> to Dad's? Blanca and I went skating in front of Mom's house after school yesterday. Sam got really mad at me because I told Mom he was throwing dirt clods at us, and she made him go inside.

Mom says that I'm confused about the skates and that I should take better care of my toys. <u>Roller skates are not toys.</u> They're transportation. What am I going to do without my skates?

Maybe when Dad sees how unhappy I am, he'll buy me Rollerblades. I'm getting sadder and sadder. Dad doesn't like to see me so unhappy—he always tries to cheer me up. Sometimes it seems like Mom doesn't even notice if I'm sad.

Dad was grumbling about taxes when he called to say good night.

Sunday, April 20

<u>Fiona Claire Jardin.</u> <u>Fiona Claire Jardin.</u> <u>Fiona Claire Jardin.</u>
Almost everyone I meet asks me about my name. I guess people think Fiona Claire Jardin is unusual, but really it's not so strange. My parents named me for my two grannies. <u>Fiona</u> is Celtic, like my mom's family—it means "fair" or "light." And <u>Claire</u>—well, that's sort of French, like my dad, for "clear." <u>Jardin</u> is French, too, for "garden."

I guess my name <u>is</u> sort of odd, if you think about it: "Light Clear Garden." Some days I feel more like a dark foggy weed patch. Dad says Irish-and-French is a spicy combination. I don't know about that. Mostly everyone just calls me Fio, unless I'm in big trouble. Then I'm Fiona Claire Jardin.

If my name wasn't Fiona, I'd want to be Martha. Or Heather. Laurel is good, but then everyone would get me and my mom mixed up. I used to sort of like the name Sarah. Annie is nice. Jacqueline? Too glamorous. Margaret? Hannah? Nichole? Elizabeth?

We beat the Bluejays yesterday, 10–7. I scored the go-ahead goal, and my mom and dad went totally berserk.

Friday, May 2

Dad stayed up all night last night to help me with my Social Studies report. We were supposed to work on it last weekend, but we forgot. (Well, Dad forgot—and I sort of forgot to remind him about it.) He spent hours working on the costume while I finished my written report. Something seemed a little odd when Dad showed it to me before I went to sleep, but I was too tired to say anything. I guess we should have checked up more on each other, because I thought the costume was really strange when I tried it on this morning. Dad said I looked great—exactly like Cleopatra. Except I was supposed to be Pocahontas.

Dad had made this fancy headdress with fake jewels all over it, and he pinned together an old tablecloth to make gold harem pants. It wasn't too bad for Cleopatra, but I didn't look one bit like Pocahontas. When I told Dad the costume was great, but could we make it look a little more like Pocahontas (because that's who I was supposed to be), he closed his eyes and started counting backwards from 100. He said maybe we should call Mom for help, but I was nervous about that idea. Mom thinks it's important to be prepared. Dad likes to go slowly, then hurry up and do stuff fast at the last minute. If one of them is right, who's wrong?

Dad said it was silly to worry about calling Mom for help. He quoted from Proverbs: "Pride goeth before destruction, and an haughty spirit before a fall." I had no idea what he was talking about, but I decided to call Mom anyway. She rushed over to Dad's and brought a bunch of feathers and beads. She had an old leather-fringed vest, too, and by the time she and Dad were done with me, I looked a lot more like a Native American princess than an Egyptian queen. (It's a good thing Mom keeps a big box of old costumes and weird thrift store clothes in the attic.)

No one knows for sure if Pocahontas actually saved Captain John Smith from being executed in Jamestown, Virginia, in 1608. But she did marry John Rolfe. And she did help to make things more peaceful between the Native Americans in the colony and the settlers. She even got to sail to England to visit King James I and the Queen. Everyone applauded for my report—even Miss Grimes.

Blanca said I was a spectacular Pocahontas. She gave her

report on Tuesday. She chose Joan of Arc, and she was totally awesome. Joan of Arc helped France win a big war against England. Some people said Joan of Arc was a witch, and she got burned at the stake when she was only 19. Other people thought Joan of Arc was kind of nutty. She said she heard voices telling her what to do, but she ended up being a saint. Being a saint must be almost as good as being a celebrity, except celebrities probably get more money. Saints just get a lot of extra credit in heaven.

Spring is really busting out everywhere. It was so beautiful today. All the dogwood trees and forsythia bushes are in bloom. I walked home from the bus stop with Natalie, and we rode our bikes down to the pond.

Mom said Katie stopped by on her bike. Mom told her I was down at the pond with Natalie, but Katie didn't come looking for us.

Monday, May 12

We played the Flamingos again tonight.

I refused to pitch, so Mr. Todd and Dad put me in at shortstop. I sort of like shortstop, except it's always so busy. Eileen Goudreau is useless at second base. She mostly worries about getting dirt on her uniform. And Erin DeMille isn't all that great at third. So that pretty much leaves the infield up to me.

I didn't know what to do when Blanca hit the ball. When she

first got up to bat, she blew the most amazing bubble with her gum. It popped all over her face. We had to stop the game so she could clean up all the sticky gunk. She must have had a whole pack in her mouth. The count was 3–0, but then Alexis pitched a good one. I knew Blanca was going to hit that ball. She slammed a worm-burner right at me. I watched the ball go into my glove, just like Dad always says to do. But then I didn't know whether to throw it to first or just sort of drop it.

Blanca's not the fastest runner. So I had lots of time to make up my mind. I decided to throw the ball to Annie Frack at first base. I kind of hoped she would miss it, but she didn't. Annie never misses anything. My throw was too good, anyway. Blanca was out. It wasn't even close. But she wasn't mad at me at all. She said, "Nice play, Fio!" Even though that was the third out for the inning.

The score was 8–7. I'm pretty sure we won, because Dad was screaming and jumping all around after the game. I don't think Dad would have been so happy if we had lost. Dad doesn't like to lose. No matter what. Neither does Mom. I don't care so much.

Katie's mom brought the snack. Devil's food cupcakes—with Gummi Worms on top!—and blue Gatorade. I snuck an extra cupcake for Blanca. When it's my turn to bring the snack, Mom always makes peanut-butter celery sticks and lemonade. She worries about spoiling everybody's dinner.

Celery and peanut butter are OK but boring. Who cares about dinner anyway? Chocolate cupcakes are way better.

Dad left right after the game. He said he was having dinner with that Sarah lady from church.

Wednesday, May 14

I'm here in the bathroom, looking in the mirror and trying to cry.

I'm thinking of every sad thing that's ever happened: Not getting the pony I wished for on my fifth birthday. Pappy Ryan dying. Getting Miss Grimes instead of Ms. Larson for fifth grade. Losing the championship soccer game last year. The Divorce. Snippers running away.

John Robert is a nuisance. Every time I talk about laughing, he wants to talk about crying. Like this:

Me: "Do you think it's weird I forgot how to laugh?"

J. R.: "Do you think it's strange you never cried about the Divorce?"

Me: "I asked you first."

J. R.: "Ladies first."

John Robert is too polite.

Me: "Don't you think it's better for a kid to laugh instead of cry?"

J. R.: "What do you think?"
Me: "I asked you first."

John Robert pulled on his beard.

    J. R.: "Is it possible that crying and laughing
    are part of the same thing—that maybe you
    have to cry before you remember how to
    laugh?"

That sounded like a trick question. I wanted to say, "Is it possible that you're a dip, John Robert?" But that would have been rude.

    Me: "Uh-oh. It's five after four. Time's up—
    Mrs. Dudley must be waiting out front.
    Gotta go!"

Saturday, May 17

I hate my life. Mom and Dad ruined it.

Me and Sam have to go to the Y's day camp for six weeks this summer. Sam thinks it will be fun because Matt and Ryan and Jason and all of his other geeky friends are going. Y camp stinks. I liked it OK when I was a little kid like Sam—I was too young to realize how stupid it is. They make you sing all these dumb songs. And you have to swim in the slimy lake and do skits every day.

Last summer I went to horseback-riding camp for two weeks.

I had my own horse. Her name was Sheba. I fed her and groomed her twice a day. Sheba's going to be looking for me this summer. I promised her I'd be back. But Mom said six weeks of Y camp costs less than one week of riding camp. So that's that.

Mrs. Dudley's going to pick us up from camp every day. Mom's going to work later on her days so she can take some time off in August. Sam doesn't even care. All of a sudden he likes Mrs. Dudley.

We're not even taking a vacation this summer. Dad says we'll spend a few weekends at the shore with Mama and Papa Jardin. That's not a vacation—it's family business. We always used to go to Cape Cod for at least one week in June every summer. Mom said maybe we could go back to the Cape next year. She looked all sad, so I didn't complain. I tore up Sam's paper airplane instead. So now I'm grounded for the rest of the day. Big deal.

Blanca has to go to Y camp, too, because her mom will be in Argentina. (Mrs. Hidalgo is a doctor, and she spends two months every summer working at a clinic near where she grew up in Argentina. Mr. Hidalgo is a chef at a fancy restaurant, so he stays here with Blanca and Francesca.) She says Y camp isn't so bad. Right. Blanca is always so cheerful. Kids are supposed to get to hang out during the summer. Summer is not supposed to be like being locked up in prison.

This S-T-I-N-K-S.

Thursday, May 22

Sometimes I'd give anything—my shell collection, my best starfish, my ant farm, maybe even Emerson—to be like Natalie Winter.

Just the sound of her name is so mysterious: <u>Natalie Winter.</u> She's 11½ but she seems older. Like 13. (She told me she did kindergarten twice because her birthday is in October. And her mom says she was too wild to start first grade when she was 6, because that's right around the time her dad left them.) We've walked home together from the bus stop a few times.

Even though we've been neighbors for six months, I still don't know too much about Natalie. She's by herself a lot. Her mother is a nurse and works the second shift, so she doesn't get home until after Natalie goes to bed, except for her days off every Tuesday and Wednesday. (I would <u>not</u> like that.) Natalie's mom lets her wear black everything—even black high-tops. And Natalie always has the most incredible lunches. Like kiwi-and-peanut-butter sandwiches on white bread. She never brings leftover Tuna Helper on whole wheat bread for lunch. And she doesn't have curly red hair and freckles. Her hair goes all the way down her back. Shiny black, and straight as a stick. Natalie's eyes are huge—like a cat's—and dreamy. She gets to walk home all alone from the bus stop. Mom always offers her a ride with us, but Natalie says she likes to walk. Even when it's raining.

Natalie is so quiet. Mom says she's shy. Sometimes I try to

talk to her at lunch. Mostly she just smiles and doesn't say much. Maybe it's lonely to be so mysterious. Once when I said something about Dad, she said she doesn't know where her dad is—she hasn't even seen him since she was 6. She said I'm lucky to have a brother. I'd let Natalie borrow Sam, but sometimes he feels like all I've got for sure. Even if he is a pest and an idiot, he's the only person I see every single day.

I dreamed the other night that Sam went to live at Dad's townhouse all the time. I stayed with Mom. I guess that sort of makes sense, because they're guys and we're girls. But I can't imagine Sam and me at different houses, no matter what. That dream was a nightmare.

John Robert says that isn't going to happen. No way my mom and dad will separate me and Sam just because they split up. But it <u>could</u> happen. I never thought my parents would get Divorced . . . but they did.

There's that full moon, floating like a big yellow balloon over the pond. We don't have school Monday, because of Memorial Day. I bet we'll go over to the Hidalgos' this weekend for a barbecue.

Sunday, June 1

Happy Birthday to me!

It's just like Mom said. When I went to bed last night, I could smell the honeysuckle. I had that funny feeling in my stomach. Like when you're waiting in line to ride the Big Dipper—you might throw up but maybe not.

I can hear Mom banging around in the kitchen. I hope she's making waffles with strawberries and whipped cream. And Tootsie Rolls on top. That's how Dad makes them when it's a special occasion.

I've never been 11 before. When I woke up this morning, I felt different. I just checked in the mirror—I look different, too. I wonder if Mom will notice that I look more grown-up. She says I can't wear lip gloss or get my ears pierced until I'm 15! My mom is old-fashioned.

My party isn't until Saturday, after Mom gets paid. Who would make a kid wait six whole days for her birthday party? We're going to Roll-a-Rama: me, Blanca, Katie, Anne Marie, Maggie, Marlane, Ramona, Dawn, and Frankie. I don't know about Natalie. We sent her an invitation, but she never said yes or no. I hope she got it. Mom said we'll call her if we don't hear anything by Friday. Sometimes it's good that my mom is so organized. She likes to make lists. Dad says that's because she's a Virgo. (But she's sort of a Libra, because she's right on the cusp. Dad thinks that makes sense, too, since Mom is super tidy and she likes to make sure everything is fair. Virgos are organizers and Libras are peacemakers—that's mom, for sure.) And Mom says Dad's a space case because he's an Aries. I'm a Gemini and I say astrology is a bunch of baloney.

I bet I'm the only one who'll have to rent skates on Saturday. That's so pathetic. Everyone I know already has her own Rollerblades.

My best birthday ever was when I was 5. That was just before

Sam was born. (I can still remember a tiny bit when it was only me and Mom and Dad.) That day they woke me up when it was still dark. The three of us drove up to the lake to see the sunrise. I don't remember much else. Except that we had hot dogs and roasted marshmallows for breakfast. And the lake was all smooth and silver-shimmery. When the sun came up, a heron flapped by us. Mom said that was good luck. Forever. She put six candles in a banana (one for good luck!) and lit them. I blew out all the candles at once.

That was one of the best days of my life—me and Mom and Dad holding hands with the sky glowing pink and orange. We spent the whole day at the lake and drove back after dark. When we got home, my parents let me stay up till midnight. We played Twister and had root beer floats. I didn't want that birthday to end.

If only we could all go back there. To the time when my mom and dad were parents together. I should have wished for everything to stay just like it was that day. But then I wouldn't have Sam. Besides, my wish didn't come true anyway. I never did get a pony.

Friday, June 6

Yea!!!

School's out and I made it to sixth grade!

No more elementary school. That's for little kids. Like Sam. In September I'll start riding the bus to Susan B. Anthony

Middle School. I'll have my own locker and will get to change classrooms and teachers instead of sitting in the same desk and listening to boring Miss Grimes all day. The school mascot is the Barracuda. I don't see what barracudas have to do with Susan B. Anthony, but Dad says maybe it's because she was so ferocious about the things she believed in. I asked him what Susan B. Anthony believed in, but he said I'd have to go look her up in the encyclopedia.

We had a big end-of-the-year assembly. Mom and Dad came together! They didn't even tell us they were coming. Sam led the whole school in the Pledge of Allegiance. At that end part he said, "with liberty and dusting for all." That's what he always says. I've told him a million times it's <u>justice</u> NOT <u>dusting</u> for all. Maybe <u>dusting for all</u> makes sense when you're 5 and still in kindergarten. (Sam gets $2 every week for dusting at Dad's house, so he kind of likes dusting.)

I got two gold certificates: one for most improved penmanship and one for good citizenship. I could hear my dad cheering and I felt a little dizzy. So I walked very slowly to the stage. Blanca got a gold certificate for school spirit. She was sort of happy. But mostly she's sad because her mom leaves for Argentina in three days. At least Blanca gets to go there for two weeks in August.

Besides going to the Cape in June, we used to go away for two weeks every August. Sometimes we'd go places where Dad had a travel feature to write. One summer we flew to San Francisco and drove from there to Yosemite. It was the most amazing place I've ever seen. The year after that we went canoeing in Minnesota. My parents promised they'd take me and Sam to France one summer—so we could see where they met. Promises don't count when you get Divorced.

Everyone was hanging around out front after the school assembly. I could tell Katie was mad. Neither of her parents had come. She got a gold certificate for leadership, except she tore it up. Katie sat on the curb with Miss Grimes, then a taxi came to pick her up. I guess having your parents together doesn't always make everything perfect. At least my mom and dad came to the assembly.

Me and Sam and Mom and Dad all went out for ice cream afterwards. Even though I was happy my parents came to my school together, it made me nervous to sit between them at Lickety Split. I kept thinking: What if Mom orders the wrong flavor or Dad burps and they get into a fight? They didn't, but I was tense the whole time. I guess I've gotten sort of used to being with each of them separately. Sometimes it just seems easier that way.

I'm glad it's summer and I'm a sixth grader. I bet everything—like Divorce and Decimals—gets easier when you're in sixth grade. Maybe I'll get to dance with Dylan now that we're in middle school.

Tomorrow I get to celebrate my birthday <u>and</u> the end of school!

Saturday, June 7

I got Rollerblades!

They're turquoise with black trim, and they're so smooth they make me feel like I'm flying instead of skating. I got all kinds of great stuff. The Rollerblades are from Mom and Dad. I got turquoise flip-flops with matching sunglasses and a beach towel from Blanca. A purple Gap T-shirt from Katie. A yo-yo from Sam. And bunches of other stuff. Granny Ryan sent me a blue Lava lamp! Natalie came skating, too. She's not so good at most sports, but she sure can skate. She gave me two calligraphy pens—one black and one purple. And she said she'd show me how to write in fancy script with them.

But the most amazing thing of all is that I got my own room at Dad's house! We had pizza at Mom's after we went skating, and I was so mad because Dad left the skating rink early and didn't come over to Mom's at all. He said he had to finish a story for tomorrow's paper. So he missed the cake and ice cream and all the presents.

Mom drove me and Sam over to Dad's because it was supposed to be his Saturday with us even though Mom organized the party. Blanca came with us, too. She's spending the night. I should have known something was fishy because usually Mom just honks the horn and waits to make sure Dad's home to let us in. But today she said she'd help carry a bunch of my presents into Dad's.

I was so angry at Dad, I walked past him without even

looking—like I wasn't speaking to him. I stomped straight to my room. But none of my stuff was in there. No bed, no desk, no dresser. Just all of Sam's stuff. I heard Sam yelling from Dad's study next door, and when I went out and opened the door to the study to see what was going on, everyone was in there and they all yelled, "Surprise!" The whole room was filled with balloons and a big banner that said: FIONA—A ROOM OF YOUR OWN!

All of my stuff was in there—I mean in <u>here.</u> Dad turned one end of the living room into his study space. He's got his desk and computer and all of his books out there. It doesn't look bad at all. Dad said that it's important for an 11-year-old girl to have her own space. (He gave me a book called <u>A Room of One's Own</u> by Virginia somebody, but I'm not sure what it's about. Dad said not to worry—I'll probably grow into that book. Mom said Dad was right about that.) Mom hung up the sign that she painted for my door. It has my name on it, and PLEASE KNOCK FIRST!

What a great birthday.

Sunday, June 8

Mom made chicken and dumplings for supper.

Mom always calls Sunday dinner "supper." I'm not sure why, but we usually eat early on Sundays. My mom is kind of a nut about Sundays. She says Sunday night sets the mood for the rest of the week. She always makes cozy food on Sundays—no frozen pizza or canned soup. Sometimes she makes turkey pot-pie. Or macaroni and cheese. Strawberry shortcake. Blackberry cobbler.

Chicken and dumplings. It used to be my favorite Sunday supper. Not anymore.

I don't remember much about the day that Mom and Dad told us they were getting Divorced. But I know it was a Sunday last year—in February, I think, because it was already dark out when we were having supper and there were still valentines all over the kitchen table. And I <u>know</u> we had chicken and dumplings for supper that day.

We were eating at the kitchen table instead of in the dining room. (We almost always did that on Sundays.) I said grace and passed the salad really fast—I was so hungry for chicken and dumplings. I ate two big helpings.

I thought Mom and Dad must have had a big fight, because they weren't talking <u>at all.</u> Sam was smashing peas and drop-ping dumpling bombs on his plate. Dad sort of coughed before he started to talk. I can still remember his mouth moving. But I don't really know what he said after "Divorce." Something about him and Mom changing, and trying hard to work things out. About how they'd always be good friends. And how they'd always love me and Sam. All I heard was "Divorce, Divorce, Divorce." Mom and Dad were both crying.

That's when the room started to spin and all those dump-lings flopped in my stomach. Then I threw up all over the kitchen table <u>and</u> all over myself.

Dad was holding Sam, and Mom was hugging me and trying to clean up the barf. Sam said, "Fio hurled!" And then he said, "What's a Divorce? Am I getting one, too?"

He's lucky he didn't know.

Dad read from The Adventures of Tom Sawyer that night because I still remember the part about Tom meeting up with Huckleberry Finn and that dead cat. Dad fell asleep right in the middle of a chapter. I could hear him snoring on the floor by my bed while I watched the moon through the tree branches. I had the worst stomachache that night. Dad moved in with his friend Paul the next week, and started looking for a new place to live.

I used to love chicken and dumplings.

Wednesday, June 11

Today John Robert and I talked about Sam. Sort of.

It doesn't seem like John Robert cares one bit about Sam. No matter what I say about anyone else, John Robert always wants to get into <u>my</u> business. Like this:

> <u>Me:</u> "I think Sam should be grounded for the rest of his life."
>
> <u>J. R.:</u> "Fio, why are you worrying about Sam?"
>
> <u>Me:</u> "Because he's my little brother. Don't you even want to know what he did? He called my mom a bad name. I'll give you a clue: It begins

with b and it rhymes with itch. Just because
she wouldn't–"
J. R.: "Do you ever get mad at your mother?"

Duh. I knew that was another one of his trick questions.

Me: "Hey, that's a ruby-throated hummingbird
there on your wall, isn't it? Did you know that
sometimes their wings beat almost 100 times a
second?"

John Robert didn't seem to care about hummingbirds, either.

Thursday, June 12

Oh boy. This is fun. Not.

Sam and I have to hang around with Mrs. Dudley all week
because Y camp doesn't start until next Monday. This morning
we had to walk all the way to the library with her. She won't let
me and Sam watch one minute of TV, even though Dad lets us.
Mrs. D. says television is R-O-T. Now she's in there cooking
something smelly for lunch. Whatever it is must be really gross.
Brussels sprouts! Hasn't she ever heard of grilled cheese or
peanut-butter-with-honey? I'd rather go to Y camp any day than
have Mrs. D. watch us.

I've been writing in this journal for six months. Half of a
whole year. Sometimes I take a break, but it's weird . . . like I've

gotten used to writing something down most days. Sometimes I write before breakfast. But usually I do it before I go to sleep. When I don't write at all, it's almost like I haven't brushed my teeth. Or like Mom or Dad forgot to tuck me in bed.

John Robert told me that surprising things happen when you keep a journal. I'm still not sure what he meant. But sometimes if I'm really mad when I start writing stuff down, by the time I'm done I'm not so mad.

I guess that is sort of surprising.

Sunday, June 15

This is the Second-Worst Day of My Whole Life.

The Worst Day Ever was when Mom and Dad told us they were getting Divorced. It was a very bad day when Dad moved over to his friend Paul's house. And a horrible day when Granny Ryan came to get me and Sam before the movers loaded up our stuff at Orchard Lane. But today was even worse. For sure I'm going to find another family that's not so messed up. I'm sick of this one.

Today was Father's Day, and Dad dropped us off at Mom's house two hours late this afternoon. Big deal. Me and Sam and Dad went to the county fair. We rode the roller coaster and the bumper cars and the Ferris wheel and the carousel. We didn't have time to call Mom. We were too busy having fun. Mom doesn't know about F-U-N. She'd rather be a grouch and worry about money all the time. We stopped at a farmers' market on the way home and bought her a basket of strawberries and some pansies for out front. Except she was <u>really, really</u> mad. She started screaming at Dad, and he yelled right back at her.

The two of them were stomping around the front yard. Sam was hanging on to Dad's leg, and Dad was huffing like a big blowfish. I tried to tell them to stop, but they wouldn't. When Dad said, "Laurel, what are you really angry about?" Mom took the basket of fruit and threw it at him. Dad's right—Mom has a good arm.

There were berries everywhere. Mom said that Dad's always traipsing off with us and having all the fun. She said she's the one who has to keep track of the orthodontist and the car pools. Then she said she can barely afford a game of Scrabble.

Dad got all puffed up like he does. And Mom got smaller and smaller. They both kept screaming, and I kept trying to pick up all the strawberries.

Then it felt like something broke inside of me. I put my hands over my ears and started yelling at them. They're Divorced now, and they shouldn't do that mean stuff to each other anymore. I started to cry and I couldn't stop.

Mom and Dad looked at me, then at each other. They seemed surprised that I was bawling, because I hadn't cried in such a long time. Mom came over and held me so tight, I could feel her heart thumping. She said, "Fio, it's going to be OK." Then she started to cry, and pretty soon Dad was crying, too. Not Sam. He was stuffing his face with smooshed strawberries.

The Cramptons across the street must think we're crazy, with all those berries flying everywhere, and me and my parents crying in the front yard. I wanted to <u>smash</u> something. Something big that Mom loves. Or something that's really important to Dad—like his stupid computer.

Then they'd know what it feels like when something you love more than anything gets smashed.

Sunday, June 29

After the Big Blowup, I took some time off from this journal.

I'm <u>sick</u> of writing about stupid stuff. I wish Sam and I hadn't gone to the fair with Dad for Father's Day. And I wish we hadn't gotten back to Mom's house so late.

I never cried about the Divorce because I <u>knew</u> that once I started I wouldn't be able to stop. I cried and slept a lot for a few days after the Blowup. Mom said maybe she should take me to see Dr. Rubin, but I knew he couldn't help. I wasn't sick. I just had some weepy-sleepy bug.

Sam didn't want to miss Y camp, but I didn't want to go <u>at all</u>. So Mom took two days off from work. She and I just messed around. I got my hair trimmed, and Mom bought me three new outfits—shorts and tops. It's a good thing we finally went shopping, because none of my old clothes fit.

Dad came over even when it was Mom's days to take care of me and Sam. He and I walked down to the pond every night and skipped rocks across the water. I can do four skips so easy now. That really makes Sam mad, because he can only skip twice.

Mom and Dad said I should check in with John Robert. But I didn't want to talk to him. Then they made me choose: Either I go to see John Robert or I start writing in this journal again. They wouldn't even let me talk on the phone to Blanca or Katie. And they said that if I didn't choose, I'd be grounded until I did.

So here I am, writing in this stupid journal just like before. I've got my tape player turned up really loud to annoy Dad. Even if I write every day for the rest of the year, it won't fix anything.

I have to pack up for Mom's. Now my new sunglasses are gone, and nobody cares one bit.

Tuesday, July 1

Natalie came over today after I got home from Y camp.

We saw her walking home from the library with a bunch of books, and I asked if she could goof around for a while. Natalie doesn't have to go to Y camp. She gets to stay home by herself all day. She can just read, or listen to music, or watch TV all she wants. Natalie seems sort of lucky, but sort of not.

Me and Sam and Natalie shot hoops until we got too hot. When we came in, Natalie went straight to the piano. When I asked if she plays, she said, "A little." She sat right down and played the most incredible music.

I said, "Natalie, that sounds like Bach!"

She smiled. "It's his <u>Polanaise in G Minor.</u>"

She said it like she was playing "Row, Row, Row Your Boat" or "Mary Had a Little Lamb." I didn't hear one mistake. Natalie said she started playing the piano when she was 4, and that music keeps her company when she's alone.

Katie rode up on her bike just when Natalie was leaving. She asked me what Natalie was doing at my house. I told her that we're neighbors . . . and friends. Katie said that Natalie's strange and she'll never be popular. She said I shouldn't waste my time on Natalie Winter.

Sometimes Katie Larkin seems like the one who's wasting my time.

Friday, July 4

I <u>told</u> Dad that I didn't want to come to the Jardin family picnic this year.

It isn't fair. Sam got to stay home with Mom. Dad made me come anyway, so I didn't talk to him all the way up here. I could hear him grouching that he was going to give away my headphones because I'm turning into a noodle-brain. Plus, he said my hearing will go bad if I listen to loud music all the time. I just hummed louder and louder. Like I couldn't even hear him. Sometimes he sneaks Bach into my tape player. Does he think I don't know the difference between classical music and ska? Doesn't he ever get tired of Bach? N-O!

I <u>do</u> like the Jardin family picnic. I have 11 aunts and uncles, and 17 cousins on my dad's side. Almost all of them gather every Fourth of July at the beach cottage. The thing is, they're all real families—with a mom and a dad and kids. All together. Except Uncle Harvey. He says he's never getting married and who needs kids when you've got 19 nieces and nephews?

I must have looked sad or mad when Dad and I got there, because Papa Jardin winked at me and whispered, "Let's bug-out for the dugout, String Bean." He always calls me that. I bet he knew I didn't want to see my cousin Lillian. She's six months older than me, and she thinks she knows everything. I haven't seen her since the picnic last year. I didn't want to hear Lillian or Beatrice, her perfect little sister, tell me it's too bad my parents split up. There's no way Uncle Phillip and Aunt Susan will ever get Divorced. They're like Mr. and Mrs. Larkin—kissy-face all the time.

Papa and I walked down the beach, all the way to the lighthouse. We didn't say too much at first. That's one of the nice things about Papa. He doesn't gab at you all the time. But then he asked about Mom. I said she seems pretty good now. She's not so sad all the time. Papa just shook his head and said, "I miss your pretty mama. She was the best darn horseshoe player in the whole family! Plus, she makes the best soda bread."

Papa said to tell Mom <u>bonjour</u> from him. I told him what John Robert says—that kids shouldn't be messengers for grown-ups. At first Papa looked surprised. Then he smiled his crinkly smile and said he'd just have to call up Mom himself. Mom would like that. She's always loved Papa. And Mama Jardin, too, and her blackberry pie on the Fourth of July. Like John Robert says, sometimes you have to work a little—and sometimes you have to work really hard—to keep love, or even friendship, alive.

Papa, Dad, and I watched the fireworks from the roof of the cottage. We were all alone. Except for the stars and the moon. I could hear the waves breaking and I saw the fireworks light up the whole sky. Like that time Mom and Dad woke me up in the middle of the night to see the northern lights.

I bet Mom and Sam climbed up on the roof, too, so they could see the sky light up above the willow tree. Mom loves the Fourth of July. She's sort of patriotic.

Wednesday, July 9

I knew Mom and Dad would tell John Robert about my crying fit if I didn't tell him first. Maybe he should be a spy instead of a therapist.

> Me: "So did my mom or dad tell you I had a
> Big Blowup a couple of weeks ago?"
> J. R.: "Did you?"
> Me: "I got so mad at them for fighting, and
> then I started to cry. I cried for two whole
> days."

And then I started to cry all over again. Right there in John Robert's office. I couldn't stop. He handed me a box of tissue.

J. R.: "Fio, why are you crying?"

Me: "Because I'm so sad?"

J. R.: "And why are you so sad?"

Me: "You know . . . I'm still sad about my mom and dad. Will I always be sad?"

J. R.: "That's a big question, Fio. I don't know the answer. It's possible that some part of you will be sad for a long, long time. But that doesn't mean all of you will always be sad."

John Robert was quiet for a minute.

J. R.: "Fio, how do you feel when you cry?"

Then it was my turn to be quiet.

Me: "Lighter?"

John Robert smiled, then he said: "Fio, this isn't a test."

Me: "I know, I know—there are no right or wrong answers!"

J. R.: "You're right about that!"

Me: "I almost always am."

J. R.: "Do you think so?"

I almost smiled. John Robert can't exactly take a joke. I'm not going to see him next month. He said he's going to California on vacation with his family, like everybody else in America—except us. (Family? I didn't know until today that John Robert has a wife and a 6-year-old daughter named Sally. It's like he's a regular person—and a dad!) So the next time I see him it will be September, after school starts. Two whole months without John Robert? I've been talking with him (and playing checkers) for more than a year. I think there's some law that you can't be friends with a therapist, but I like John Robert anyway.

I've never gone to middle school before. What if I can't get my locker combination to work? John Robert told me not to worry. He said I'll figure it out. I guess I have to trust John Robert. He's kind of old, so he knows stuff.

Sunday, July 13

That Howard guy came to dinner.

I guess he wasn't a wrong number, but he is bad news. His jeans are so clean and stiff looking, he must iron them. Mr. Howard Clean Jeans. That's what Sam and I call him. I don't know where my mom found him. She says he's an architect, like Michael. He sure seems like a doofus to me. He swirls his hair around the back of his head. Like that's going to cover up his bald spot. Plus he has a mustache. It wiggles like a caterpillar. And it makes him look suspicious.

Mom tied her hair back with a red ribbon. She put on lipstick and nail polish to match. I forget that Mom can be sort of pretty. Especially when she smiles. She laughed at everything Howard said. Even when he asked her to pass the salt.

Mom spent all afternoon cooking: barbecued chicken, scalloped potatoes, sugar snap peas, and peach pie. Howard ate every bite. I wasn't one bit hungry. Sam asked Howard to toss the Frisbee around. Now they're all out back playing croquet and laughing. Why is Sam pretending to have fun? He doesn't like strangers. And Howard Dork is definitely <u>strange.</u> (Maybe Mom gave Sam his allowance in advance so he'd act like he was having fun.)

It's a lot more fun playing solitaire in here with the blinds closed. Maybe I'll sneak a tiny piece of pie. The peaches are our first ones from the tree out back. Sam and I picked them.

Friday, July 18

We had the all-camp talent show at the Y this afternoon.

Today was the end of the second two-week session. I still complain about going every morning, but camp isn't really so bad. I'm the director for the talent show and Blanca is the choreographer. It's almost like we're junior counselors. And Max—he's the head counselor—says that when we're 14 Blanca and I can really be junior counselors. Max is so C-U-T-E. <u>He's 16!</u>

I've been reading <u>Anne Frank: The Diary of a Young Girl.</u> It's on my summer reading list. Anne Frank was a Jewish girl who hid with her family in an attic in Amsterdam during World War II. They were hiding because Adolf Hitler and the Nazi guys wanted to kill all the Jews. Anne Frank and her family hid in the attic for more than two years. They never went outside. She was only 13 when she started her diary.

Anne Frank loved movie stars. She dreamed about going to Hollywood, but she never went. The Nazis found her family, and she died in a concentration camp. She was only 16. Like Max.

Anne Frank called her diary Kitty. She always wrote "Dear Kitty," like she was writing to a friend. When I put my journal next to Anne Frank's diary, my life doesn't seem so hard.

Tuesday, July 22

Dad picked me up early from Y camp.

I felt sort of yucky after lunch. Max couldn't get ahold of Mom at work, so he called Dad. I was afraid Dad would be mad, because it's not his day to take care of me and Sam. But Dad was working at home today, so he came right over to camp. He said I was being silly—he's my father every day, not just Wednesdays through Fridays and every other Saturday.

That's true, but I can't believe he brought me over to Mom's house. He called and left her a message that he'd stay with me until she gets home. Mrs. Dudley is going to pick up Sam. I didn't even know Dad had a key to Mom's house. He said they traded keys a long time ago, in case of emergencies—and I thought I was the only one with keys to both houses.

Dad keeps coming in to check on me. I don't have a fever or anything. Dad says maybe I got too much sun. Maybe he's right. It was 103°F at noon. I drank two glasses of juice when we got to Mom's, and I do feel better. It's strange to think of

Dad sitting in Mom's living room reading a magazine. He seems so big in this little house.

Mom just got home—it's only 3:15. She must have gotten Dad's message. I hope she's not mad at Dad for being here. I don't think so. She just said, "Martin, thank you so much for picking up Fio." That's what she said, "so much." Mom brought me some ginger ale and a cool washcloth for my forehead. Now they're in the kitchen and Mom's making tea.

Their voices sound nice together. I'd forgotten about that.

Friday, July 25

Sam and I skipped camp today.

Dad took the day off work because it's Sam's birthday. I got him a great slingshot. I can't believe Sam is 6 years old. Sometimes he acts like he's about 3. I remember the day he was born. At first I wanted Mom and Dad to give him to Uncle Harvey. But after they let me hold him, I decided we should keep him.

We had hot fudge sundaes for breakfast. Dad lets us do things backwards on our birthdays. Sam's party isn't until tonight, after Mom gets off work. We're going to the mall so that Sam and his goofy friends can play video games and throw pizza at each other. Gross! Dad gave Sam a pretty package from Sarah. It's a model biplane—how did she know he's nuts about model planes?

We borrowed Matt's little two-wheeler this morning and took

it to the park. There's this grassy hill there, and Dad kept hold-ing the back of the bike while Sam rode down. After about 100 times, Dad let go of the bike halfway down the hill, but he didn't tell Sam. When Sam looked back, Dad was way behind him. Sam couldn't believe it. (John Robert says trust isn't so much of a problem for some 6-year-olds. Kids like Sam believe their moms or dads will always be around to hold the bike steady.) He kept pedaling and riding and yelling: "Yo, Daddy! I'm riding a bike!" Dad just stood there and smiled, real proud.

I was proud, too. And a little sad. I know Mom would be so happy to see Sam on a two-wheeler. All by himself for the very first time. I wish I'd had my camera, but I can't find it any-where.

Too bad Mom wasn't there to see Sam's face.

Tuesday, July 29

Blanca slept over last night. (We carpool to the Y every day anyway, so Mom just took us from here this morning.)

We grilled halibut and made s'mores, then stayed up late watching for shooting stars and chasing fireflies. Sam caught a bunch in a jar, but I let them all go after he went to sleep. Maybe he'll forget about them. He's sleeping on the couch be-cause Mom said Blanca and I need our privacy.

Blanca and I snuck some cookies, a box of Cocoa Puffs, a carton of milk, and chocolate syrup. We mixed all the gunk together. Blanca called the goop Train Wreck. It looked like a mud slide to me. It didn't taste too good, either.

We were getting scared telling spooky stories, so I said we should talk about something else. Blanca got real quiet. She said she never thought that my mom and dad would get Divorced. Then she asked me why they did.

I thought for a long time, but I told her I still don't know the answer. For a while I thought maybe Divorce was contagious, like the chicken pox. Maybe they caught it from Andrew's parents. Or from Mr. and Mrs. Henry. But my mom and dad said no—Divorce isn't contagious.

Sometimes I try to remember when Mom and Dad started fighting all the time. It seems like Dad was traveling for work a lot. And me and Sam kept Mom so busy every day. When Dad wasn't working on a story, he just wanted to hang out with me and Sam and Mom at home. He likes to watch the Phillies and the Eagles on TV. Mom was always with us, so sometimes she wanted to dress up and go out—just her and Dad. They both said something about drifting apart, except I never felt like we were drifting. Not until after they got the Divorce.

Blanca asked me what the worst part is when your parents split up. (Best Friends get to ask questions like that. They're not being mean, just curious.) I told her that the very worst part is never having everyone together all at once. It's like you're trying to do a big, hard jigsaw puzzle with 1,000 pieces, and the one piece you need to finish the puzzle is missing.

Blanca said it's kind of like that when her mom goes to Argentina every summer. Except she knows that her mom will always come home to them. Blanca said she thinks the worst part would be Mrs. Dudley. Mrs. D. isn't really so bad, even if she is totally wacko. For one thing, she's a great tap dancer. When I told Blanca that, she laughed so hard her glasses fogged up. Then she started snorting like a pig, and milk squirted out of her nose. She kept saying, "Mrs. Dudley? Tap-dancing in those shoes?!" And then she laughed even harder.

Blanca and I made a promise that if we ever get married and then get Divorced (no way!), we'll find each other. And all of our kids will live with us in a big house with a porch swing. Daffodils. Lilacs. A huge tree fort. And a creaky attic. Kind of like the Old Lady in the Shoe. Except there will be us two girls, and Melville and Emerson—and all of our babies.

Saturday, August 2

Sam fell asleep in my bed.

That's OK. He had a bad day. For one thing, his slingshot disappeared. He thinks Mom took it because he hit her with a huge spitball. Mom says she didn't touch Sam's slingshot. He and I hunted and hunted for it, but we can't find it. He was mad because Dad wouldn't rush over after work to help us search.

When we went to the library this afternoon, there was an old man and a little boy standing out front. The boy was about 5 or

6, like Sam, except he was really skinny. He wanted Sam's yo-yo, and Sam let him try it for a few minutes.

I checked out a book about Argentina and Sam got four lizard books. When we came out, that old man and the boy were still there. The man was wearing a long parka, mittens, and a Redskins beanie, even though it was almost 100 degrees out. He had a scraggly old sign: WILL WORK FOR FOOD—PLEASE?

Sam asked Mom why they wanted food. She said they're probably homeless. Mom gave the man two dollars and Sam handed the boy his yo-yo. I couldn't think of anything to give them, but I sort of waved good-bye. The old man said, "God bless you and your nice kids, lady."

Sam's been worrying about that little boy all night. We played about 20 games of crazy 8s, and I think he felt better. Now he's asleep. He asked where the kid's mom and dad are— and what would happen if our mom and dad ran out of money and we got "hopeless" like that boy. That's how nightmares get started, so I said Sam could leave the desk lamp on. Just this once.

I don't mind so much. Blanca left for Argentina this morning for more than two weeks, and I already miss her. When I sat down to breakfast this morning, there were two cut-paper angels under my cereal bowl. (Mom just smiled mysteriously when I found them.) They were connected to each other by their wings. One halo said FIONA, and the other one said BLANCA. Blanca had drawn hearts all over the back, and she wrote: "Fio, don't forget your very best friend. I will miss you. Sincerely,

Blanca Lucia Galvez Hidalgo." By now Blanca should have found the blank journal I slipped in her backpack.

John Robert is gone, too. And Katie is leaving for Cape Cod next week. At least we're done with Y camp and Mom's taking some time off. I'm glad to have Sam and Natalie to fool around with and help fill up the quiet. I told Sam that the man and the little boy are <u>homeless,</u> NOT <u>hopeless.</u> He said, "Whatever."

I guess I'll just sleep in Sam's bed. I wish he would wake up so he could help me worry about that homeless man and the little boy.

Thursday, August 7

For some reason I was in a really bad mood today.

I got in a big fight with Sam after lunch and ripped up his comic book. When Mrs. Dudley tried to pull Sam off of me, I told her to mind her own dumb business. Before she sent me to my room, she looked at me kind of cross-eyed and asked what was wrong. I didn't want her and Sam to see me cry, so I came in here and slammed the door.

I can't think of anything to do for three hours till Dad comes home. I called Natalie, but her phone just rang and rang. Where is she? It's so hot and boring in here. When I stopped crying, I opened this journal so I could hurry up and get my writing over with. I looked at the blank page and realized I've been mad all day. Dad didn't have breakfast with me and Sam this morning, like he usually does before he goes to work. He didn't even tell us that Mrs. Dudley would be here when we woke up.

Dad always says that I need to learn to "go with the flow." Right. He'd freak out if Sam and I weren't here when he got home from work. Especially if we didn't leave him a note or anything. At Mom's house we have a big grease-pencil board that says TODAY. We try to write things down on it so we all know The Plan every single day. Dad thinks that's a lot of fussiness, but maybe we should try it with him, too.

I'm 11 now, so I'm going to tell Dad what I think. That's what John Robert says to do. I'll talk to Dad right after dinner. Maybe.

Monday, August 11

Watch out!

This is scary. Mom's in the shower with a plunger and some bent pipe she keeps calling The Snake. She turned on the garbage disposal after dinner, and the next thing there was zucchini and cherry pie coming up from the drain in the shower. Sick! Sam asked if she'd given herself one of those oatmeal facial things again. He said he'd call Dad for help. Mom frowned and told him to put down the phone and get the bucket—fast.

The stuff in the shower smells really B-A-D. And it looks like chewed-up tofu. Mom said she didn't know that the garbage disposal and the shower are hooked together somehow. Sam said maybe we'd better not turn on the TV, just in case. Mom said not to worry—she's pretty sure that plumbing and electricity are separate.

I wonder how Mom learned to work a plunger. Maybe she took a class when we were at Dad's one night. Maybe good old Mr. Howard Clean Jeans taught her!

Saturday, August 16

Dad is <u>ruining</u> my life.

Stephanie Flanders asked me over to spend the night. Dad called her mom back and asked if Stephanie could come here instead. He's going to Pittsburgh on assignment next week and he'll miss two days with me and Sam. So he really wants me to stay home with him tonight. Mrs. Flanders said she would worry too much about Stephanie if there wasn't a mom in the house—so could I go over there?

Dad went totally ballistic. He told Mrs. F. that he used to be the backup Girl Scout leader. Plus, he's certified in CPR. <u>And</u> he makes me and Sam eat green vegetables and fresh fruit every day. That's all true (if pickles count as a green vegetable), but Mrs. F. didn't care. I kept telling Dad to calm down. He said Mrs. Flanders should be ashamed for assuming things about him just because he's a guy. When I started to cry, Dad hung up the phone and told me to go to my room. At least I have my own room now, with a door that locks. It sounds like Sam's doing somersaults or cartwheels in the hallway. He thinks it's hilarious when I cry.

Dad's pacing around the living room and crabbing at Sarah on the phone. I bet he's mostly mad because he lost his favorite harmonica, and he thinks Sam and I must have been fooling around with it. Just because he's spaced out doesn't give Dad the right to ruin my entire life. How could he do this to me? Stephanie is the most popular girl in my whole class. She has <u>green</u> eyes, and her shoes always match the color of the clothes she's wearing. She looks like she belongs in the Delia's catalog.

Dad can be such an idiot. That must be where Sam gets it. Maybe Mom could call Mrs. Flanders to explain about Dad. How he gets kind of wound-up sometimes. But what could Mom say to make her not worry?

Stephanie called back and invited me over for next Friday night instead. That's when Dad will be away, but now I don't know if I want to go.

Monday, August 18

Every time there's a full moon something unusual happens.

Now my purple rhinestone barrettes are gone. Sam probably threw them away. He was bugging me, so I said I was going to tell Mr. Bartleby that the garbage disposal doesn't work anymore because Sam poured a bucket of papier-mâché down it. Sam got all scared and begged me not to tell. I just laughed at him, and now he's in our room crying. Sam <u>hates</u> it when I make him cry.

Mr. Bartleby is our landlord. He's always snooping around,

and I know he doesn't like kids. Mom said he worries about peanut-butter fingerprints and broken windows. Why doesn't he worry about important stuff—like babies with AIDS or protecting the rainforest? We didn't have a landlord on Orchard Lane. Mom and Dad owned our old house, and they used to let us roller-skate around the kitchen. They didn't care one bit about fingerprints. Sometimes Mom even skated with us, and Dad used to walk up the back stairs on stilts!

When I asked Mom why we don't buy this house, she made a fierce face and said we can't afford it. We used to have money to do lots of great stuff. I want to get a job, but who will hire an 11-year-old? Mom says I can't even baby-sit for real until I'm 12. When Mom runs out of money, Sam always tells her that she should just write a check. Yeah, right. Sam doesn't get the connection between checks and money in the bank. (I didn't understand how money in the bank works, either, until I was 9 or 10.)

Natalie's spending the night. We rented the movie Grease, and she's bringing over some of her mom's old clothes so we can dress up like the Pink Ladies. When you get to know her, Natalie is really funny. She sure can do the jitterbug. Me and Natalie and Mom are going to bake chocolate chip cookies and make a big banner because Blanca and her mom come home tomorrow! Sam promised to leave us alone. Mom brought two new snake books home from the library to keep him busy.

I get to go to the airport with Mr. Hidalgo and Francesca to pick them up.

Wednesday, August 20

I spent the night at Blanca's last night.

She looks like she grew a whole inch taller, even though she was gone less than three weeks. We stayed up talking until after 11:00. I told her all about the mess with Stephanie Flanders and about watching <u>Grease</u> with Natalie. She told me about her cousins and the little village where her mother teaches. When it's summer here, it's winter in Argentina. Isn't that cool? Blanca goes to Argentina every summer to visit her mom. I'm saving up to go with her when we're both 16.

I'm so glad Blanca's home. I feel kind of lopsided when she's gone. That's how it is with best friends.

Sam and I are staying at Mom's house, because Dad won't be back from Pittsburgh until Friday. He's doing a story about some discus thrower who's really mad because she can't compete against guys in the Olympics.

Friday, August 22

Blanca's having an end-of-summer slumber party tonight!

It's just going to be me, Katie, Anne Marie, Maggie, and Blanca. We've all been together since kindergarten. Our moms used to call us the Five Musketeers.

I can't decide what to wear. Maybe the new jeans and the top Dad brought me from his trip. But I might save that outfit for the first day of school. I could wear my new plaid skirt and turquoise T-shirt. Or maybe I should wear my purple sweats, because the nights are starting to get kind of chilly.

I'm supposed to get my hair cut tomorrow, but maybe I should just get my bangs trimmed. Or should I grow my bangs out? Then I'd look more like Katie. Her hair is all one length. Blanca's hair is all one length, too, except she has feathery bangs. Anne Marie mostly wears French braids—she can braid her own hair without even looking! Maggie's hair is layered, kind of short. That's good for her because she's so sporty. I used to <u>hate</u> having red hair, but lots of people tell me I'm lucky. Now I don't mind so much.

Blanca said her parents are making an Argentinean feast for dinner. That means Mr. Hidalgo will burn steak on the grill. I'll just eat a lot of <u>papas,</u> or potatoes, instead. Mr. and Mrs. Hidalgo always make chicken for me, anyway.

I hope middle school isn't a disaster.

Saturday, August 23

Katie got a B-R-A!

That's the first thing I noticed at Blanca's slumber party. You could tell Katie was kind of embarrassed—and proud, too. I can't believe she didn't tell me she had gotten a bra. It's her business, but she didn't have one last week when we went bowling. So what's the deal? She's just showing off. She always has to be the first one for <u>everything.</u>

Blanca said her mom bought her a bra, too. She's not as

bouncy as Katie on top, and she hasn't decided whether to wear her new bra on the first day of school. And I was just trying to choose between jeans or my plaid skirt! <u>Duh.</u>

Maybe I should get a bra. Just in case. Maybe not. My mom doesn't even wear a bra half the time. When I asked her why she doesn't, she said she's not so sure it's necessary—for her. Maggie said H-E-L-L will freeze over before she'll wear a bra. (Maggie always says just what she thinks. Even H-E-L-L. Not me. I'd be grounded for a year if I said that.)

We started soccer practice today. Blanca and Katie are on my team, and—surprise!—Dad's our assistant coach. Our first game is September 6.

Tuesday, August 26

We always come up to the lake for a few days the week before Labor Day.

Pappy Ryan used to come here with his father. He helped Great-grandpappy build the cabin. Pappy died when I was 7, and Granny Ryan hardly ever comes here anymore. This time I got to bring Blanca and Natalie along for four days. Mom's taking them home when Dad comes up on Thursday. Mom was sort of nervous about asking Granny if Dad could come up here, but Granny knows Dad loves the cabin more than anyone. I'm crossing my fingers and toes so that Dad won't ask Sarah to come up for even one day.

Yesterday Blanca and Natalie and I caught 14 tree frogs.

Those frogs made such a racket before we let them go. Sam kicked over the bucket in the kitchen, and they went hopping all around the cabin. We caught most of them, but one croaked at Mom when she got into bed last night. Mom can really scream.

I thought the lake and the cabin would seem different this year. I was sort of scared to come up here, but Mom said not to worry. She was right. I have much worse stuff to worry about—like getting Mrs. Withers for my sixth-grade advisor. Linda Miles had her last year and told me all about her. <u>She said Mrs. Withers might be a witch.</u>

Everything at the cabin is just the same. The mattresses are lumpy, and the water pump creaks and clanks. It's chilly in the morning until Mom gets the woodstove going. Mr. Minnelli comes over almost every morning for coffee and flapjacks. He's <u>still</u> a big grouch. Today he told Mom, "That Divorce business is a bunch of hooey!" Guys as old as Mr. Minnelli know what they're talking about.

I'm sort of glad that Mr. Minnelli is still a grump—and that the lake is fr-r-r-eezing. Like always. The tips of the trees are just starting to turn red and gold. Just like last year. And the year before that.

I was glad that Blanca didn't wear her bra. (Natalie started wearing one last year. She says she matured early. No kidding.)

Sunday, August 31

Now I've got my own room at Mom's house, too!

While Sam and I were still up at the lake with Dad, she had a carpenter put up some folding wooden doors to close off the little sunroom from the living room. She painted the room the same lemon-drop yellow with blue trim as our room—<u>my</u> room—and moved all of Sam's stuff in there. And she put up his posters and set up his desk and bed and the rest of his junk.

I don't know who's happier, me or Sam. But Mom said Dad was right—it's important for me to have my own private space.

I can't wait to start middle school.

Monday, September 1

The last time I looked at the clock it was 11:45.

There's a new moon, and it's really dark out and quiet. Sam went to sleep at eight, and Mom must be asleep, too. She hasn't checked on me since before ten o'clock.

No wonder they call it <u>Labor Day.</u> I know the holiday is supposed to celebrate all people who work, but maybe it should be a special time for kids whose parents make them run around the day before school starts. Mom and I went shopping for a bra. It took about three hours, but we finally found one that sort of fits. Size 28AAA. But it feels scratchy, and it looks all bumpy under my T-shirt. I put it in my bottom drawer so Sam won't find it. Under all of my sweaters. Maybe I'll save it till next year.

I got my school supplies organized. And I helped Sam label his pencil box and all his other stuff. I took a bubble bath and washed my hair three times, and I've got my clothes for tomorrow hanging from the door frame. I decided the plaid skirt and the turquoise top will be good. My haircut is a disaster, but Linda Miles says I can wear my Gap cap until the first bell rings for homeroom. Mom said maybe I can get new shoes next month.

What if Blanca and I don't have any classes together except homeroom? What if <u>Dylan</u> and I don't! What if I get Mrs. Withers? I'll do <u>anything,</u> as long as I don't have that witch for advisor. I'll scrub my retainer every night. I'll set the table without being told. Now it's 12:07. School starts today!

I can't believe Sam's in first grade.

Tuesday, September 2

This is incredible!

I am so lucky. Mrs. Withers got her license to be a bus driver and decided to quit teaching. My advisor is a girl from Louisiana—I mean, she's a <u>woman.</u> Her name is Jasmine Evangeline Teresa Jefferson Dupré, and she's my Language Arts teacher, too. She said we can call her Miss Dupré or Jasmine Dupré. She said her father always calls her Jasmine Dupré when she's in trouble, which is most of the time! When she wrote her name in cursive on the blackboard, it stretched across the whole thing, as long as the Mississippi River: MISS JASMINE EVANGELINE TERESA JEFFERSON DUPRÉ. She said that her last name has a "cute" accent over the é. I've never known anyone with an accent before. Below her name she wrote: DAUGHTER/SISTER/FRIEND/TEACHER/POET/MUSICIAN/ADVENTURESS.

Miss Dupré has dozens of tiny braids, with shimmery blue, green, and purple beads at the ends. And three little gold hoops in each ear. Her eyes sparkle like black diamonds. She just moved here from New Orleans—except when she says it, it sounds like "Narlins." For a minute I thought I was in the wrong class—I kept looking for Miss Withers. But Miss Dupré looked right at me and said, "You must be Fiona Claire Jardin." How did she know? (Mom said she must have studied the class photographs from the three elementary schools that promote fifth graders to Susan B. Anthony Middle School.)

The very first thing during homeroom, Miss Dupré had us push our desks into a circle. She said that being part of a circle makes everyone feel more connected. Katie looked kind of nervous and moved her desk over near the door. (Sometimes she's not so good at "going with the flow," as Dad would say.) Natalie moved her desk right next to Miss Dupré's, and I moved mine next to hers. (Natalie is always brave.) Then we had a class meeting.

Miss Dupré told us that we'll be talking about a lot of different things during homeroom. She also said that as our advisor, she's interested in whatever each of us wants to discuss, privately or as a group—whether it has to do with school or home or anything else. Then Miss Dupré said that because Language Arts is our first period after homeroom, we won't waste any time getting started every day.

Miss Dupré got quiet for a minute. She said she has a plan. This is it: We all have to write two pages in a journal two nights a week for homework. We can write about the subject she assigns each week, or about any topic we choose. Except we can't write about the same thing twice. She said that until Martin Luther King Jr. Day—that's not until January!—all of our journal entries or essays have to be handwritten in ink. No computers.

Miss Dupré said that writing in ink takes commitment. She believes that when you write with your hand, in ink, you write from your heart. She said that when you use a computer, you're writing from somewhere else—like your left elbow or your right ear!

Most of the kids didn't seem to know anything about writing in a journal, but I do—sort of. Sometimes it's scary to write from your heart. You never know for sure what you're going to say. Katie looked confused. And very tense. Now I'm glad Mom and John Robert made me start a journal.

Another good thing: Miss Dupré said that writing in our journals can count for one of our two Language Arts essays each week. We just have to copy parts that are OK for her to read.

I've never had a teacher like Miss Dupré before. She's nothing like Miss Grimes. Katie thinks she's weird. (It's only the first day of school, and Katie said she might transfer to Miss Waverly for advisor and Language Arts. That's probably because Dylan has Miss Waverly.) Katie doesn't like to try new things. For example: She has grilled chicken and boiled rice for dinner almost every single night. How boring! Katie would never eat cheese enchiladas or teriyaki salmon.

Blanca and Natalie think Miss Dupré is very cool. Me, too. When she talks, it sounds like she's singing.

Thursday, September 4

Here's my schedule:

7:30–8:00	Homeroom/advisory (Miss Dupré)
8:05–9:00	Language Arts (Miss Dupré)
9:05–10:00	Social Studies (Mrs. Hanley)
10:05–11:00	Science (Mr. McCready)
11:05–12:00	Art (Mr. Winship)
12:00–12:30	Lunch
12:35–1:30	Math (Mrs. Casey)
1:35–2:30	Phys. Ed. (Mrs. Douglas)

At the end of Language Arts today, Miss Dupré asked if anyone had any questions. Mary-Megan Chandler poked her hand up a little and asked if "Narlins" is part of the United States! Miss Dupré laughed and said it sure enough is. She pointed to the U.S. map and said New Orleans is just about the finest city in Louisiana—maybe the finest city in the whole country.

Then Joseph Tucker asked Miss Dupré how old she is. She laughed again, then said a lot of people think it's rude to ask a woman her age. She said she likes to keep her age a mystery. She did give us one hint, though. Miss Dupré said she has five braids for every year since she was born. And then she laughed some more and shook her head. Those pretty beaded braids clicked and clacked a little. It made me dizzy trying to count them all, but I'm going to figure out how old Miss Dupré is before the end of the semester.

I asked the last question, right before the bell rang—I wanted to know how Miss Dupré ended up in Wilmington, Delaware, at Susan B. Anthony Middle School. She said that she and Mrs. Hanley were college roommates at Tulane University in New Orleans. Mrs. Hanley told her about this school—and all about Ms. Harris, the principal, and her interesting approach to education. Ms. Harris flew all the way down to New Orleans to watch Miss Dupré teach, then she offered her a job.

Miss Dupré said she's always lived in the South, and this seemed like a good chance for her to find out about life north of the Mason-Dixon line. She said she and Mrs. Hanley have lots of ideas about teaching Social Studies and Language Arts together.

The only thing Miss Dupré is worried about so far is where to find fresh crawfish! I told her I don't know about crawfish, but you can buy really good fresh crabs down on Market Street.

Saturday, September 6

We won our first soccer game of the season this afternoon. The score was 7–3.

Dylan rode his bike over to watch. He looks different. It's like his nose got really big over the summer and he has all these zits. We're not in any of the same classes this year. He's got Miss Waverly for advisor. Dylan whistled every time Katie kicked the ball. I don't mind so much. He looks kind of dorky. Besides, all of a sudden Jamil got really cute.

We played the Killer Cyclones. I didn't score any goals, but Dad says that's not really my job, since I play sweeper on defense. Dad loses his voice every game. Sometimes I wish he didn't yell so much, but he says that's part of his job as a coach.

Who would name a soccer team the Screaming Jonquils, anyway? Dad thinks the name confuses and scares other teams, but I don't get it. Katie scored four goals. She's a super kicker. Her mom and dad were cheering and jumping all around. It must be nice to be an only child so you can have your parents all to yourself. Especially if your mom and dad stay married. Katie doesn't have to ask for two copies of stuff from school like I do—one for Mom and one for Dad.

Blanca can't figure out why I like soccer so much. She plays right fullback. Mostly she just hunts for four-leaf clovers and straightens her socks. She thinks it's important to look good at all times. Not me. I like to move and to really launch the ball with a good kick.

Natalie refuses to play soccer. She doesn't like to get sweaty.

Wednesday, September 10

I barely even recognized John Robert today!

He shaved off his beard and got contact lenses. (His eyes are all blinky and squinty. He kind of reminds me of Emerson.) It's only been two months since I last saw him, but he looks like somebody else—like a college guy. Maybe that's what happens when you go to California for a few weeks, like he did with his family.

I guess John Robert thinks I seem different, too. He shook my hand and acted very formal. Almost like he forgot I'm just a kid and we've been friends for more than a year.

J. R.: "Fiona, how are you?!"

Me: "Well, I'm in sixth grade now and I have a locker. We won our first soccer game of the season. Katie got a B-R-A, and so did Blanca!"

J. R.: "Really, and what do you think about that?"

Me: "Uh . . . I figured out my locker combination the very first day of school. And my advisor is named Miss Jasmine Evangeline Teresa Jefferson Dupré. She's my Language Arts teacher, too, and we're learning all about poetry this semester."

J. R.: "Poetry—well, what do you know?"

Me: "I know that a haiku is a poem about nature. Most people think haikus are about syllables, but Miss Dupré says they're really about sounds—seventeen different sounds: five in the first line, seven in the second, and five in the third. Haikus are beautiful but tricky. I wrote one!"

J. R.: "Is that right?"

Me: "Absolutely. I call it 'Mud':

> *Spring rain*
> *Puddles in pools*
> *Sleek slime.*"

J. R.: "Very nice."

Me: "I'm working on a cinquain: five lines— two, four, six, eight, and two syllables each. Miss Dupré is amazing!"

J. R.: "I see. And what about you, Fiona—how are YOU?"

At first I didn't know what to say.

Me: "I'm good. I mean—I'm doing well."

I was kind of surprised to hear myself say that.

Thursday, September 11

Miss Dupré said that so many kids were asking her questions after class about Louisiana and her big, long name, she decided to tell us a few things about her life.

She said she was born in a place called Plaisance, Louisiana. It's about 100 miles west and north of New Orleans—just northwest of Opelousas, which is north of Lafayette, which is west of Baton Rouge. (What a lot of weird-sounding names.) She said that her great-grandma, all four of her grandparents, and lots of aunts and uncles and cousins still live in Plaisance, and she loves to go there—especially if she's feeling a little blue and wants some zydeco music to pep her up. Miss Dupré said zydeco reminds her of gumbo, because it's loaded with good things: fiddle, accordion, trumpet, guitar, bass, drums, saxophone. Zydeco reminds me a lot of ska. Gumbo is a spicy Louisiana soup loaded with chicken and sausage and seafood.

Then Miss Dupré wrote her name on the blackboard again: JASMINE EVANGELINE TERESA JEFFERSON DUPRÉ. She said her name is sort of like gumbo, too. She said she ended up with two first names because her mom wanted to call her Jasmine but her dad liked Evangeline—so she got both names when she was born. She chose Teresa for her confirmation name (for Saint Teresa and because Mother Teresa is one of her heroes!). Jefferson comes from her mother's family, and Dupré is her father's surname. She said her family's roots in Louisiana go back more than 200 years—and that her cultural heritage is a spicy stew of African American, West Indian, French, Acadian, Spanish, and Anglo-Saxon. Royalty, slaves, pirates, merchants, bankers, dance hall ladies—Miss Dupré said her family's history is loaded with all sorts of rascals and colorful characters.

Miss Dupré said sometimes names are like blueprints or maps of the past. She also said that sometimes names don't have much to do with who you are. For tomorrow, we all have to find out three things about our name.

That's easy—I already know all about my name and what it means. Mom and Dad have been telling me about it for as long as I can remember.

Friday, September 12

Names are so interesting.

Katherine (that's Katie's real name) comes from the Greek word for "pure." Katie said that makes sense because she's "pure" English through and through—Larkins on her dad's side and Winthrops on her mom's. Natalie is French or German from the Latin word for "to be born." Everyone laughed when Joseph said Tucker is an English name for someone who works cleaning cloth—he's Joseph Dry Cleaner! Johanna is a variation of Joan or Jane, girl forms of John, from the Hebrew for "the Lord is gracious." Eamon is Old English for "prosperous protector" or "holy warrior."

Miss Dupré said Jasmine is Arabic or Persian for "a flower," and that Henry Wadsworth Longfellow made up the name

<u>Evangeline</u> when he wrote a poem about a broken-hearted Louisiana girl who waits and waits for her boyfriend to come back to her. <u>Dupré</u> is French for "dweller of the meadow."

<u>Fiona Claire Jardin</u>. Irish and French. "Light Clear Garden." I didn't have to do one bit of research about my name. I just flipped back in this journal to April 20 to make sure I remembered everything.

cnikrof eirod corèit —that's what my name looks like in the mirror!

Saturday, September 13

My left foot is totally useless.

Sometimes I don't even know why I have a left foot. We had a bye today, so we practiced instead. We worked on dribbling, passing, and shooting for two hours straight. Coach Davies says my left foot is going to make all the difference in soccer for me from now on. She said that for the next few weeks she doesn't want me to use my right foot at practice—but I <u>am</u> supposed to use it during games!

I can do almost anything with my right foot. Dribble, scoop under the ball, pass. And when I shoot with my right foot, the ball always goes where I want it to. My left foot is like a dead lump at the end of my leg. No matter how hard I try, I always flub up when I try to do anything with it.

Dad says Coach Davies is right: If I'm going to get a soccer scholarship to college, I've got to get my left foot going. I don't know about that. By the time I go to college, I'll probably be able to clone my right foot and just put it on my left leg.

That would be awesome.

I have a math test on Monday. Mrs. Casey says two weeks is enough reviewing—it's time to move beyond multiplying decimals to three places. Uh-oh.

I don't think I'll ever be able to write a cinquain. So far I've only got one line:

Oak door

Miss Dupré says that sometimes it's good to start a poem with a concrete image in your head. (Not <u>concrete</u> like a side-walk, but <u>concrete</u> like clear.)

Tuesday, September 16

I told Sam and Mom that it was a rotten idea to leave that message on Dad's answering machine.

Sam said something like, "Dad, don't worry. Dr. Rubin says my arm will be better in six weeks. Besides, it's my right arm, so I can still write. Ha-ha, get it? <u>Right and write?!</u>"

I thought maybe it would be better to <u>show</u> Dad that Sam's OK in person. Mom said no, she'd rather just leave a message. She kept walking around in circles. I said I'd tell Dad it wasn't her fault that Sam broke his arm. He shouldn't have tried to dive from the top of the piano over to the couch. The dumb thing about being 6 is that sometimes you really believe you can fly.

It didn't work out that way. The emergency room was creepy, just like on TV. Especially with Sam bawling and his wrist bone poking out of his skin. But he got this totally cool neon-orange cast. I was the first one to sign it! Then Mom drew a great dragon on it. Maybe Dad will write him a poem.

Blanca's sleeping over. We found my old Magic 8 Ball in the back of the hall closet. When Blanca asked, "Does Dylan like Fio?" it replied, "Don't count on it." When I asked, "OK, does Dylan like <u>Katie?</u>" the message was, "Yes. Definitely." I tossed the 8 Ball back in the closet. Who cares about Dylan and Katie anyway?

The moon is full tonight. See—strange stuff happens every time there's a full moon.

Monday, September 22

Today is the autumn equinox—day and night are the same length.

It's also Mom's birthday! She's 37. She looks lots younger. Like around 35. Sam made her a bookmark with his picture on it. Mom reads <u>a lot,</u> and she's always forgetting what page she's on. Granny Ryan gave her a Phillies sweatshirt, size XL. (Granny must think that Mom is still going to grow some more.) Uncle Will sent a book about Ireland. And Aunt Kathleen sent her a smelly candle that's supposed to help her relax.

(Aunt Kathleen has gotten a lot of goofy ideas since she quit her job at the bank in Philadelphia and moved to Oregon. She's going to school to be a masseuse. Granny says she's lost her marbles.) Aunt Shaun sent fuzzy pink golf-club covers. Mom's trying to figure out what to do with them. She says Aunt Shaun should be a professional golfer instead of an accountant. Aunt Shaun doesn't know that Mom sold her clubs.

Dad gave Mom a roll of canvas. He drove over here to give it to her—all wrapped up with flowered paper and ribbons. Maybe that sounds sort of dull, but I think Dad gave Mom canvas because he loves her paintings so much. Mom made chicken cacciatore for dinner and asked Dad if he wanted to stay. Last year Dad was staying at his friend Paul's house on Mom's birthday, and he didn't even call or give her a card. This birthday was a lot better. Dad had a glass of wine with Mom, but he didn't stay for dinner. Mom sent some chicken home with him.

Howard called to wish Mom a happy birthday, but she just let the answering machine pick up. He sang "Happy Birthday" to her on the tape. He has a terrible voice.

Maybe it's a good thing Snippers isn't around—she'd howl if she heard Mr. Clean Jeans sing.

Sunday, September 28

Me and Mom and Sam changed the oil in her car today.

Mom got oil all over everything, but she was really excited. And the car didn't even blow up when she started it. It took us about three hours because Mom had to read a bunch of books about what to do, and she kept going inside to wash her hands every ten minutes.

Sam said Mom should just call Dad to come over to change the oil. Mom growled at him and said no way. When I said maybe Howard could help, she said, "Howard?" Like she'd never heard of him. Then she said, "Oh, Mr. Clean Jeans! I'd rather do it myself. Howard's such a dork." No joke.

Mom said we saved $30. She was so happy. It seemed rude to ask her how much all of those books and wrenches cost. I didn't say a word. We went out for frozen yogurt and then walked down to the pond to fly kites. Blanca came with us. She has this great dragon kite.

It's only three months until Christmas. Will Sam and I go to Mom's house or Dad's? We need to make a plan.

Saturday, October 4

Sam's sleeping over at Matt's tonight.

I hope Sam's OK. He's never spent the whole night at a friend's, except for at our cousins'—and they're family, so that doesn't really count. I wonder if he'll crawl around under Matt's bed before he climbs in. Sam says that's the only way he knows for sure that there are no monsters under there. Mom and Dad always tell him it's silly to do that, but I sort of know what he means. Sometimes it's better just to make sure. At least Sam doesn't hide under his bed when he's mad anymore.

Now he just goes out and jumps around on his pogo stick. That sounds like one of John Robert's ideas.

Dad fell asleep on the couch, so I made dinner. It isn't easy to make dinner when you're not allowed to turn on the stove by yourself. I made tuna sandwiches and celery sticks stuffed with peanut butter. I set the dining-room table with Mama Jardin's lace cloth and napkins. And two candles. With me and Dad at each end of the table. Very elegant. Dad was so surprised, and he let me light the candles. He especially liked the celery. I started to wash the dishes after dinner, but Dad wouldn't let me. He always reminds me that I shouldn't try to be the mom. (Mom always tells me and Sam not to try to be the dad at her house.)

Dad and I worked on my history project after we finished cleaning up. I'm trying to build Mount Vernon to go with my report about George Washington. Dad says that maybe Mount Vernon is too big for us to build, but I don't think so. Katie's doing her report on Thomas Jefferson. Mr. Larkin is building an exact replica of Monticello. Katie's mom is sewing tiny curtains and bedspreads. The Larkins are a major pain.

Wednesday, October 8

John Robert and I played checkers today for the first time in a really long time.

The thing is, we had talked for a while about school. And a little bit about Katie and Natalie, and about taking care of your

109

friendships. And then there wasn't much else to talk about, even though we had 20 minutes left. That's when he said, "Fiona, how about a game or two of checkers?" And then he set up the checkerboard on his desk. He was humming and smiling a little—all innocent.

He said he wanted to be red. (He almost always lets me be red.) Then he beat me three games out of four, and every time he'd take one of my kings, he'd say, "A-ha!" and flip my black checkers in the air. Like he was really glad to clean my clock. John Robert must have practiced a lot since the last time we played.

I wonder if he set me up? No, he wouldn't do that.

Thursday, October 9

I set the alarm clock for really early this morning so I could study for my Social Studies test some more.

It was still dark out when I got up, but Dad was already in the kitchen, drinking tea. The whole kitchen table was covered with pictures—mostly old pictures of him and Mom. Dad tried to gather them up so I couldn't see, but there were too many of them. I asked him what he was doing.

At first he laughed, like he was going to tell a joke. But then he got all quiet. He said, "I was thinking about your mom and me." When I asked how come, he was quiet again, and then he told me that he and Mom got married 15 years ago. I totally forgot that yesterday was their anniversary! They got married in a little church in the south of France. Mama and Papa Jardin and Granny and Pappy Ryan and everybody were really mad that Mom and Dad got married without them. But Dad said he and Mom were so in love, they just couldn't wait to get married. Besides, they didn't want a big wedding with a lot of fuss. They wanted to get married in France to remind them of where they'd met and fallen in love.

I didn't know what to say or think. I thought maybe Dad was going to cry. But he just packed up all the pictures and tied them together with a red ribbon. Then he said, "Time for breakfast, missy-loo!" He said he'd make me his Special Killer Salsa Omelet.

Sometimes when my dad wants to change the subject, he tells a joke or says something silly. I said cornflakes and juice would be just fine for breakfast. Then I asked Dad if he ever gets sad or scared. At first he didn't say anything. Then he asked, "Fio-bean, have you ever acted brave and happy when you felt scared and sad?"

Right then the teakettle started to whistle, so I didn't have to answer Dad's question. He poured hot water into a mug, then he winked at me. "Promise me you won't tell your mom I use tea bags instead of loose tea. OK, Fio? She'll think I'm a lazy bum."

Dad never answered my question, either—about being sad or scared. I never thought he could be scared of anything, but maybe he is sometimes.

The Social Studies test was impossible. I couldn't remember

one thing about the Industrial Revolution—except that James Watt did <u>not</u> invent the steam engine, like everybody thinks he did. Too bad I forgot who really invented it. If you ask me, Mrs. Hanley is overly enthusiastic about Social Studies.

Sunday, October 12

I baby-sat for the Alexander twins this afternoon.

Mrs. Alexander brought them over here so Mom could help, since I'm not 12 yet. But I was in charge, and Mrs. Alexander paid me three dollars to play with Charlie and Lily. They're almost 2 and very busy. Especially Charlie. He never stops. Lily doesn't say much, so Charlie talks for both of them. Lily has an amazing left foot, though. She kicked Sam's little football clear over the back fence. She should play soccer.

I don't really want to play the saxophone anymore. I'd rather just practice the piano and maybe get really good, like Natalie. Besides, I'm always too busy. I've got soccer practice and a game every week. Piano lessons after school on Tuesdays, and practicing every night at Mom's. Plus an hour or two of homework <u>every night</u>. I never have time to goof around.

But I don't know what to tell Dad. What if he's disappointed in me? And if I tell Mom I want to quit the sax, she'll just say, "I told you so."

Tuesday, October 14

Katie transferred out of Miss Dupré's class.

Her parents came to school yesterday and had a conference with Ms. Harris. Katie called me last night to tell me she was switching to Miss Waverly's class. She said she thinks Miss Dupré is strange and talks too fast.

Miss Dupré spoke to me in private for a few minutes during advisory this morning. She said she knows that Katie and I are good friends, and she wanted to make sure that I was doing OK in her class. Miss Dupré also said she had hoped that Katie would stick with the class until semester break, but Miss Dupré and Mr. and Mrs. Larkin decided it was better to make a switch sooner instead of later. Miss Dupré said it's always best to confront a problem honestly, and to work together to figure out the best possible solution. She said Miss Waverly is a terrific teacher, and that she will push Katie to do good work.

Miss Waverly is a big bore compared to Miss Dupré.

You can buy all kinds of things for lunch in the cafeteria—pizza, hoagies, chef's salad, soup, burritos. Mom gives me lunch money one day a week and so does Dad.

I like middle school a lot. So far.

Friday, October 17

Tomorrow is Natalie's birthday. She's the first one of my friends to turn 12.

Mom helped me pick out some sheet music for her. Plus, we got her bubble bath and soap that has lemongrass in it. She loves all of that kind of stuff—anything that feels nice and smells good.

Natalie isn't exactly having a party. She asked if I could come over for the afternoon. She wants me to bring my saxophone so we can play duets. (She doesn't know that I stink.) Then me and Mom are going out to dinner with her and her mom. Sam and Dad are going bowling, and I'm going to sleep over at Natalie's. Me and Natalie and Mom and Mrs. Winter are going to Alouette. It's the fanciest restaurant in town. The menu is in French! My mom and dad used to go there to celebrate their wedding anniversary. (They both love to eat snails.) But I've never been. We're going to get all dressed up and take a taxi.

Natalie said she didn't want to have a big party. She's just glad her mom is taking the night off and that the four of us get to do something special.

My mom says Natalie is very mature for her age. I guess so. She sure is smart—and she's funny.

Dad made red beans and rice for dinner tonight. With a tossed salad and French bread from the bakery around the corner. He said Miss Dupré had handed out copies of her favorite Louisiana recipes at Back-to-School Night last night, along with an outline of all the things we'll be covering in Language Arts for the rest of the semester. She told the parents all about our poetry project. Dad brought home my packet of works-in-progress. He liked my "found" poem a lot:

Mom's Shopping List

> *lettuce/cucumber/scallions*
> *green beans*
> *potatoes??? tomatoes celery carrots broccoli*
> *apples, oranges, bananas*
> *bread/bagels*
> *butter, milk & eggs/yogurt*
> *brown sugar*
> *chocolate chips*
> *Cheerios*
> *raisin bran   <tuna*
> *motor oil*
> *aspirin*
> *Band-Aids*
> *floss*
> *bleach>paper towels>>>>soap-soap-soap x 3*
>
> *DRY CLEANER'S, POST OFFICE, BANK!!*
> *Hardware store?*
> *Fio's cleats to XMJ*
> *Sam to YMCA by 2:30 Saturday*
> **call Mother**

Miss Dupré said the thing about a found poem is that you can't change even one letter of it. If this was <u>my</u> shopping list, I'd add cookies, popcorn, and ice cream, for sure. Too bad my cinquain isn't going so well.

Whooeee—red beans and rice are good and spicy!

Wednesday, October 22

I told Dad the truth tonight after our saxophone lesson.

I told him I want to quit—that I really don't like playing the saxophone. All that blowing gives me a headache, and when I play, it sounds like a sick elephant. When Dad blows, it sounds smooth and silky, like a turtledove.

Besides, I kind of like playing the piano now that my left hand goes so much better. Natalie has shown me lots of new things on the piano. And Mom was right—practicing makes playing a lot better. I guess that's why Coach Davies makes me work so hard with my left foot, too. Playing the piano is a little like soccer—when I really get moving, my fingers fly over the keys like they know where to go, and I get to follow along.

I'm learning a minuet by Bach. I've been working on it for two months. I guess I am like Dad, because now I love Bach's music so much. It's hard, but Natalie says it's not impossible. I thought you had to be old—at least 15—to try to play Bach. But Natalie is only 12, and she can play lots of his music.

Natalie says Johann Sebastian Bach didn't have the greatest childhood. (It seems like tons of famous people had a hard time when they were kids.) He always had music around him, because his dad was in a band. And he must have had plenty of kids to play with, because he had seven older brothers and sisters. But Johann Sebastian's mom and dad both died before he was 10, so he had to go live with one of his older brothers.

Dad got his wrinkly worried look when I told him I wanted to quit the saxophone. He said our sax lesson is our own special time each week, and he's sad to give that up.

I know what he means. It's always me and Sam and Dad. Or me and Sam and Mom. Sometimes I feel like whichever one Sam and I are with, we're all one big octopus—except with twelve tentacles (and three heads!) instead of eight. I hardly ever get any private time with Mom or Dad anymore. Maybe Dad and I could join a dad-daughter team and go bowling once a month. Maybe Blanca and Mr. Hidalgo would like to bowl with us.

I wonder if that red hairbrush Sam found under Dad's bed when he was looking for his Frisbee is Sarah's. I'm going to ask Dad about it.

John Robert says to speak up when you're worried about something.

Tuesday, October 28

Some days are like the Black Holes that Mr. McCready told us about last week.

Like today. I can hardly remember anything that happened.

Nothing special. It seems like a big blank. I got up. Went to school. Came home. Mrs. Howard was late for my piano lesson. Then Natalie came over to do math homework, and she stayed for dinner. We had spaghetti. Again. And fruit cocktail out of a can. Mom never used to feed us anything out of a can. (I used to like fruit cocktail when Mom wouldn't let us have it. But it's <u>so</u> gross.) Now Mom's reading <u>The BFG</u> to Sam—he loves Roald Dahl. And I'm in here writing in this journal. Again.

Sometimes it seems odd that the days feel so boring. But sometimes boring is OK. This time last year, when Mom and Dad were fighting and getting Divorced, I never thought that even one minute of one day would feel sort of normal.

Mrs. Howard said I'm ready to have a piano recital, and we should start thinking about what music I want to play. I am getting better, but a recital? I told her maybe we could think about that after the holidays.

Friday, October 31

Trick or treat!

I've never seen so much candy. Sam and I have it all lined up on the floor in his room. First we went to all the townhouses near Dad's (except for the Henchleys' next door—they are so M-E-A-N), then Dad took us over to Mom's neighborhood.

Sam was a flying saucer. Dad got him all hooked up with flashing lights on a battery pack, and he borrowed Dad's little tape player to make sound effects. Sam looked great, but he couldn't move much. I was Cleopatra, which was perfect—I finally got to use all that stuff Dad made last spring when I was supposed to be Pocahontas. Everyone said I looked just like Cleopatra, Queen of the Nile. Dad was so proud because he'd made our costumes all by himself. Mom was a little mopey, though. She thought we looked way too wild. (Every Halloween she still hopes I'll be a lamb and Sam will be a bunny. Sometimes Mom's so old-fashioned, it's like she's from the Little House on the Prairie. Dad says she's just sweet and traditional.)

I didn't turn in a Language Arts essay today. I couldn't think of anything to write about last night, and the assigned topic was too hard: 10 Ways to Help Save Planet Earth.

Maybe Miss Dupré won't notice.

Monday, November 3

I thought for sure it would rain today.

My mom and dad got Divorced last year on November 3. That's when the Judge said the Divorce was final. It rained buckets that day. I thought it would always, always rain on November 3. But when I woke up today, the sun was shining. I didn't even need a sweatshirt.

Miss Dupré asked me if I was OK during Language Arts. She said I seemed kind of far away. I told her I just felt like having a quiet time. She said it's good to listen to your feelings. That's dumb. How do you <u>listen</u> to a feeling? Later on when we were reviewing this week's vocabulary words, Miss Dupré said she wanted to talk to me across the hall in the computer lab.

The lab was empty, and when we sat down, Miss Dupré asked if I had forgotten to turn in my essay last Friday. I could feel that big lump that sticks in your throat when you try not to cry. I swallowed hard and told her that I hadn't forgotten—I just didn't have anything good to write about last week. She said I know the rules: "If you can't think of anything, you have to write about the assigned topic, just like everybody else." I lied and said I'd forgotten about that.

I did try, but I couldn't think of 10 ways to help save the planet. I could only think of one way to make life on Earth better: Make Divorce against the law. I tried to talk with Dad about my idea on Friday morning, but he said to hurry up—he's always in a rush to get to work. Dad said I was being childish, that sometimes Divorce makes a bad situation better. He said there are some things I'm too young to understand.

Miss Dupré and I talked until the bell rang and it was time for me to go to Social Studies. I told her that my parents got Divorced one year ago today. Then she told me the saddest story about how she felt so lost after her mom died when she was only 12. She and her three little brothers moved to New Orleans, because her dad got a job teaching at Tulane University. What a horrible thing about her mom dying. I guess I'm sort of lucky. At least my mom and dad aren't dead. (No way—they're always in my business!)

Miss Dupré reminded me that I could turn in stuff from my

journal instead of an essay. She said she wouldn't take any points off for being late this one time. I said I'd think about it. I <u>did</u> think about it and decided to copy a few pages from this journal.

Miss Dupré smiled when I turned them in after school. Sometimes I wish she wasn't quite so energetic. Then maybe it would be easier to count her braids.

Wednesday, November 5

I guess Miss Dupré sort of liked the pages she read.

She said during advisory that the October 22 entry about quitting the saxophone was "moving." Moving? (She plays the saxophone!) She also said it was wise for me to be honest with my dad and to speak up about what I was feeling. Miss Dupré said lots of adults are too scared to say how they really feel about things. I hope that part about Bach didn't remind Miss Dupré about her mom dying. That might make her sad all over again.

Miss Dupré asked how long I've been keeping a journal. I told her I started it the very first day of this year. She nodded and hummed a little. Then she said that she has an idea. And she asked if I would think about letting her read other parts of my journal.

I said maybe, but I don't know. What's her idea? John Robert asked me a long time ago if I wanted him to read my journal. He's nice and everything, but I said no way. He might be a spy for my mom and dad. But Miss Dupré can't be a spy. She's only talked to my mom and dad once, for a few minutes at Back-to-School Night. She doesn't really know anyone in my whole family, except me.

John Robert says that sometimes it helps to share secrets that make you feel nervous inside. Maybe if I let Miss Dupré read this journal, the butterflies that still flutter around in my stomach will rest for a while.

We're studying human anatomy and reproduction in Phys. Ed. for the next two weeks. Mrs. Douglas makes hormones and menstruation sound like lots of fun. I don't think so.

Friday, November 7

Dad had to pick Sam up from school this afternoon because Sam threw up in the cafeteria at lunch.

Dad thinks it's the flu. He took Sam's temperature and it's 101.2. Under the arm. Maybe it was the corn dogs and Chee•tos and the rainbow Jell-O with marshmallow whip that made Sam puke. (He said that's what he had for lunch. Mom never lets Sam buy his lunch. She says he doesn't make good choices when it comes to food.)

Dad's making chicken soup. What's he doing with the soy sauce? (I wish he would just call Mom for her chicken soup recipe.) Dad's wearing one of Mom's old aprons. She always used to wear that apron when she made Irish soda bread. I liked the way flour would swirl around her in a big cloud. She's so busy now that she has a job, she hardly ever bakes bread anymore. Dad's got a bunch of books scattered around the kitchen. I don't think Sam cares about the soup. He's asleep on the couch with a barf bucket next to him on the floor. Maybe the soup will make Dad feel better.

Dad asked what Sam and I think about having Thanksgiving up at the lake. It's a good idea. I love Thanksgiving on the lake. Mom's going down to Granny's with Uncle Will and Aunt Lily and little Emily and Molly. She said Dad could take me and Sam up to the cabin, and that Sam and I can spend Thanksgiving with her next year. That sounds fair. Last year we had Thanksgiving dinner at the Country Inn. Just me and Mom and Sam. It was horrible. Mom said she didn't feel like wrestling with a big turkey. She wanted to have a quiet holiday, because everything was so hectic when we were getting ready to move. I don't think Mom felt very thankful last year. I didn't, either.

I don't want to go to Granny's. I love her, but she always makes me and Sam take a rest in the afternoon.

Just because grannies need to rest doesn't mean kids do, too.

Wednesday, November 12

I was the tiniest bit worried John Robert might be jealous if I let Miss Dupré read this journal.

<u>Me:</u> "You know, I've never let anyone read my journal."

J. R.: "It's yours, Fio. That means you get to decide what to do with it."

Then I was quiet for a minute.

Me: "I think I might let Miss Dupré read it?"
J. R.: "You don't need anyone's permission, Fio—do you want Miss Dupré to read it?"

As soon as he asked that question, I knew the answer.

Me: "Yes. I do."
J. R.: "And do you know why that might be true?"
Me: "Not really. But Miss Dupré said she has an idea about my journal. I'm not sure why, but I trust her."

Then J. R. was quiet for a minute.

J. R.: "It sounds as though Miss Jasmine Evangeline Teresa Jefferson Dupré is a special person in your life, Fio. Trust is important—for all of us."

At first I thought John Robert wanted me to tell him that Miss Dupré is special. And that my trusting her is important, too. But John Robert didn't say one more thing about her.

John Robert is right—I do trust Miss Dupré. Tomorrow I'll let her borrow my journal for one night.

Friday, November 14

Miss Dupré remembered to return my journal today.

She was waiting for me out front before school started. She was kind of quiet when she gave it back to me. She said my journal is "extraordinary"—and then she thanked me for letting her read it. Extraordinary?

Miss Dupré asked if I had read anything that had been helpful when Mom and Dad were splitting up. I told her that I had gone to the library to check out some books about divorce. (She told me that divorce is just a regular old word, so you don't have to capitalize it. Duh. I should have known that already.) There were lots of books listed in the computer catalog, but I didn't want to ask the librarian for help. (I already have too many people snooping in my business.) My mom read me and Sam a book about two skunks getting divorced. Sam liked the story, but I thought it was stupid. Who'd want to be married to a skunk, anyway?

Miss Dupré said her best friend back in Louisiana is getting divorced, and that her friend's 13-year-old daughter is having a tough time. Her friend's name is Johnston Allen, and his daughter's name is Chloë. She asked if maybe she could copy my journal and send it to Chloë LaRue Allen. She said Chloë might really appreciate having a friend like me—even if we do live 1,200 miles apart. My heart started to thump, and I said I'd have to think about it.

Chloë. What a cool name. (Miss Dupré told me that Chloë

has two dots over the letter <u>e</u>. She said that symbol is called an
<u>umlaut,</u> and it means you pronounce each vowel separately
when two vowels turn up together—so Chloë rhymes with
<u>snowy.</u> Maybe everyone in Louisiana has strange accents in
their names.)

Chloë La Rue Allen

Wednesday, November 19

Sam quit school today.

The whole first grade went to the museum to look at old
bones. Except Sam forgot his permission slip. Dad signed the
form last week but forgot to give it to Mom to send to school
with Sam this morning. So Sam didn't get to go. He had to
spend the whole day with the kindergarten kids because his
teacher couldn't get in touch with Mom or Dad.

No wonder Sam says he's never going back to school. Now
he's tearing the house apart because someone swiped his silver
yo-yo. Mrs. Dudley's on the phone with Mom. Sam gets so mad,
sometimes I think he might spin into outer space. I hope not.
John Robert says I can't be responsible for Sam, but he <u>is</u> my
only little brother. Maybe I'll make him a fluffer-nutter sandwich and help him do his <u>Weekly Reader.</u>

I let Miss Dupré copy my journal. She gave it back to me after school and said she was going to mail it to Chloë Allen

<u>today</u>. Just think, it could be on a bus or a plane tomorrow, on its way to New Orleans. Weird!

Melville is looking sort of chubby. She needs more exercise.

Monday, November 24

I have to give my poetry presentation tomorrow in Language Arts.

I'm nervous just thinking about it. Joseph Tucker always shoots spitballs at whoever is talking. Natalie recited a poem by Maya Angelou today, and Joseph got her right between the eyes. He never gets caught. Maybe Miss Dupré needs glasses.

I shouldn't be too nervous because my speech is about Emily Dickinson. She's my favorite poet and I know all about her. Emily Dickinson grew up in Amherst, Massachusetts. I've been there a bunch of times, because that's where my dad went to college, and sometimes Sam and I go back with him to visit. She started writing poetry when she was just a kid like me. She wrote from her heart, just like Miss Dupré always tells us to do.

Emily D. wrote hundreds and hundreds of great poems (actually, 1,775 in all), some of them on scraps of paper. She didn't care about getting her poems published or about being famous. She probably would have died of embarrassment if her poems had been published when she was alive. (She died anyway, because she had a bad kidney.)

As she got older, Emily Dickinson got more and more shy.

She always wore white dresses, and she hardly ever left her house. She must have had so much great stuff going on in her head, she didn't need to go anywhere for fun. But I wonder if she got lonely, even though she had a brother and a sister.

It was hard to choose which poem to recite, but I really like #288:

> *I'm nobody! Who are you?*
> *Are you nobody, too?*
> *Then there's a pair of us—don't tell.*
> *They'd banish us, you know.*
>
> *How dreary to be somebody!*
> *How public, like a frog*
> *To tell your name the livelong day*
> *To an admiring bog!*

Emily Dickinson. I bet she knew she was Somebody way before everybody else did.

Tuesday, November 25

I've been thinking about Chloë LaRue Allen reading my journal down in Louisiana.

Louisiana is a long way from Delaware. (I got out the <u>Rand McNally Road Atlas</u> last night and mapped out how to get there. South through Delaware, Maryland, Virginia, North and South Carolina, Georgia, then west through part of Florida,

Alabama, Mississippi, and into Louisiana.) I wish Chloë Allen's parents weren't getting divorced. Maybe they should try harder to work things out.

I've got to hurry up because me and Sam and Dad are driving up to the cabin right after school tomorrow. It's a half day, so we'll be at the lake in time for dinner—if the traffic isn't too horrible. We don't have any homework over the long weekend!

What if Chloë doesn't like my journal?

Thursday, November 27

I love Thanksgiving!

Except that I ate too much mashed potatoes and turkey. And a mountain of stuffing. But no sweet potatoes or creamed onions!

Sam and Dad spent all afternoon building a pirate ship to sail on the lake. Then Dad and I made pies—pumpkin and pecan. We used two forks to make the crust. (Mom just uses her fingers to blend the shortening and flour.) I had a huge piece of pumpkin pie and gobs of whipped cream. (I do not eat pecans—or any other nuts.) The pie was OK, but not as good as Mom's. No offense.

Sam and I snapped the wishbone after dinner. He ended up with the big piece, so he got to make a wish. When I asked what he wished for, he said, "You know." 10,000 wishbones won't make Mom and Dad get back together. John Robert says it's important to see things how they are instead of how you think you want them to be. Sometimes I wish John Robert would take a hike.

Dad and Sam and I built a fire and roasted marshmallows after we cleaned up. Sam always lights his marshmallows on fire, then he eats the crunchy black part and throws away the rest. Dad read us two chapters from <u>Treasure Island</u> by Robert Louis Stevenson. Sam fell asleep right here by the fire.

Next year, when we have Thanksgiving with Mom, she'll read to us from <u>Little Women</u> by Louisa May Alcott—like she always does. Dad says there could have been a really great book if Robert Louis Stevenson and Louisa May Alcott had ended up on a desert island together back in the 1880s. Mom says that's a goofy idea. Even though they both wrote at about the same time, Louisa May Alcott was totally American—and Robert Louis Stevenson was Scottish.

Tomorrow is Katie's birthday. She thinks it's a gyp, because she always has to have her birthday party some other time when everything's not so hectic—on account of the holiday. Some years her birthday is on Thanksgiving Day. Katie thinks everyone in America should be thankful that she was born 12 years ago.

I got her a cool mood ring, even if she does always think about herself before anyone else.

Saturday, November 29

We got back from the lake this afternoon, and Katie is spending the night.

She said she really liked her mood ring, except that it turned muddy as soon as she put it on. She put it right back in the box. When Katie saw this journal on my desk, she wanted to know why I've been writing in it all year and what I write about.

I smiled and acted mysterious. It's mean to tease Katie, but sometimes she's a big snoop. She hates it when she's not the first one to try something. She even said I'm lucky, because I have Sam and two houses to hang out in. She thinks Dad's townhouse is so cool. I never thought in a million years that Katie Larkin might think I'm lucky! She said Miss Waverly is dumb and boring. She's sorry she transferred out of Miss Dupré's class, but her parents won't let her switch back.

After we turned out the lights to go to sleep, Katie asked me who I like better—her or Natalie. She said if I like her better than Natalie, maybe she'll ask her parents to take me to the Cape with them next summer. Sometimes I don't know why Katie just can't leave things alone. (Mom says she likes to stir things up for some reason.) If I told Katie I like Natalie better, she'd say mean things about me to all the kids at school. (She already told Stephanie Flanders that I have to see a "shrink." That's what she calls John Robert. Mom says calling a therapist a shrink is rude.) Natalie would never ask me a question like that. She never says mean stuff about anyone.

I didn't answer Katie's question. I made snoring noises, like I was asleep. I've known Katie a lot longer than I've known Natalie. But I like Natalie better.

Natalie Winter is my second-best friend.

Dad's picking me and Sam and Katie up for church in the morning. We have to practice for the Christmas pageant for two hours every Sunday for the next four weeks. Mrs. Howard is directing the pageant and playing the piano.

Tuesday, December 2

I guess Miss Dupré doesn't need glasses after all. She sees everything.

Today it was Joseph Tucker's turn to do his poetry presentation. I was a little surprised because he chose Langston Hughes, and I like his poems a lot—even though I <u>don't</u> like Joseph Tucker. Joseph was supposed to recite "Dreams," except Miss Dupré asked him to take the daily attendance form down to the principal's office first. When Joseph left the room, Miss Dupré said, "How many of you have been hit by Joseph's spitballs?" Everyone except Mary-Megan raised their hand. (Mary-Megan's presentation isn't until tomorrow.)

Miss Dupré said, "Very interesting." Then she said, "Well, lookee here—a whole box of straws. I'm going to tie my shoes now. I guess I won't notice if a student or two borrows a straw to use for a few spitballs." And then she bent down and untied the laces on her fancy shoes, so she could tie them up again.

Every single kid—all 22 of us, including Mary-Megan—grabbed a straw and started chewing up paper. <u>Fast.</u> We were all quiet, in our seats, by the time Joseph got back.

Miss Dupré said, "Thank you, Mr. Tucker. Are you ready now?"

Joseph walked up to the podium, and as soon as he started to say the first line, we opened fire on him! Joseph turned bright red. Like a persimmon. He forgot the whole poem.

Miss Dupré told Joseph to go back to his desk. Then she gathered up all the straws and said there will be no more spitballs in her classroom. She said, "Is that clear?"

Joseph said, "Yes, sir—I mean <u>ma'am.</u>"

She said we will all look forward to hearing about Langston Hughes tomorrow.

Miss Dupré is awesome. Today I counted 97 braids, but I didn't know what she was talking about when she asked me to give her an example of a gerund.

I still haven't made any progress on my cinquain.

Sunday, December 7

Dad was really grumpy when he dropped us off at Mom's.

Dad says he's not a Sherpa and it's ridiculous for me to haul so much stuff around. Then he said that Sam's got stuff at both houses and <u>he</u> doesn't take everything he owns back and forth.

So what? Sam's only 6. He doesn't know what it's like to be 11 and not have your favorite tapes or your hair stuff when you need it. I'm not supposed to spy, but I heard Mom and Dad talking in the kitchen. Mom said it's not my fault I have two homes. She said she and Dad should make it easy for me and

Sam to go back and forth instead of hard. Then she said that Sam and I are like snails that carry their houses on their backs—except we have backpacks instead of shells.

I always take the comforter Mama Jardin made with me to Mom's and Dad's. I sleep better with that quilt wrapped around me, wherever I am.

I haven't heard from Chloë Allen in New Orleans. Maybe she hates my journal. Maybe she thinks I'm totally pathetic.... Maybe Chloë LaRue Allen is pathetic.

Monday, December 15

Only 10 more days until Christmas!

I'm not so nervous about it anymore, just excited. Mom's taking me and Natalie to the mall this afternoon. She won't drop us off, but she said we can shop on our own for an hour while she looks for a few presents.

Mom is in a really good mood. She loves Christmas, except for last year. I asked if all four of us—me and Sam, her and Dad—can go out for pizza on Wednesday so we can make plans for Christmas. Mom looked surprised, and her left eyebrow twitched like it does when she's nervous. But she said OK and offered to call Dad.

I can barely remember Christmas Day last year. We still had boxes all around because of moving. Mom couldn't find any of our decorations, so we made paper snowflakes and garlands, and hung them everywhere. Granny Ryan was hovering over me and Sam, clucking like a hen. Mom cried all day. I kept waiting and waiting for Dad to come get us so we could have some fun.

Sam and I got lots of stuff, but I forget what.

67 braids. That's how many I counted on one side of Miss Dupré's head before the bell rang. Twice that would be about 135, which would make Miss Dupré 27. Maybe. (Joseph Tucker says so far he's gotten up to 123 before losing count.)

Wednesday, December 17

Me and Mom and Dad and Sam got Christmas all figured out at dinner tonight.

We're going to spend the day with Dad on Christmas Eve and then go to the children's service with him at five o'clock. Mama and Papa Jardin and Uncle Harvey are coming to watch me and Sam in the pageant. Mom and Granny Ryan are coming, too.

Dad's going to take me and Sam over to Mom's for dinner after the pageant, even though it's supposed to be Dad's day with us. (I bet Dad's nervous about seeing Granny and the other Ryans. I'd be nervous, too, but they won't be mean to him. Besides, Mama and Papa Jardin and Uncle Harvey are coming to dinner, too.) Sam and I are spending the night at Mom's on Christmas Eve. That way we'll be there for Christmas brunch with Granny Ryan and everybody. Mom promised she'll make Irish soda bread just for me. And sticky buns for Sam.

Dad will come get us in the afternoon, then we'll go back to his house for dinner with all the Jardins. It sounds kind of busy, but at least this year we all know what's going on.

The Christmas lights were twinkling like little stars all over downtown. We went to a new Italian restaurant for dinner instead of to the Pizza Kitchen. Dad had said we were going to a nice place, so Sam brushed his hair without being told. He even wore a shirt with a collar and a sweater. I wore my black velvet jumper, and Mom wore her new black velvet skirt with a fancy white blouse. She wore the pretty pearls Dad bought her for their 10th anniversary. She hasn't worn those pearls in a long time.

The restaurant was really nice. It's called Il Dolce, and it has white tablecloths and real flowers on the tables. Sam ordered pizza, but I had angel hair pasta with shrimp and lots of garlic. We all had double-chocolate gelato for dessert. Yum! Mom and Dad were so nice to each other. Dad hung up Mom's coat for her and helped her in and out of her chair. He was very polite. Mom told Dad she liked his story in last Sunday's paper. It was about some rich lady who turned her mansion into a halfway house for teenagers in trouble with the police.

Mom and Dad told us about the year Mom tried to roast a goose for Christmas dinner and Dad had to put the flames out with a fire extinguisher. Granny Ryan said to rinse the goose off so they could eat it anyway. Mama Jardin said she'd make a quiche instead. Mom and Dad started laughing so hard, everyone in the restaurant looked at us.

We must have seemed like a normal family. I guess no one realized the truth about us. When the waiter brought the bill, he bowed and told my dad, "You have a lovely family, sir. Merry Christmas!"

I started to say something about being divorced, but Mom smiled and squeezed my hand under the table. Dad said maybe dinner at Il Dolce should be a family tradition every Christmas season. Mom tried to split the bill with him, but Dad wouldn't let her. She just said, "Thank you, Martin, for a lovely dinner."

Friday, December 19

Just five more shopping days!

Here's what I'm thinking:

Mom—bubble bath or adjustable wrench? $14.00

Dad—ChiaPet $11.00

Sam—pirate hat and eye patch $10.50

Papa Jardin—Nolan Ryan rookie card (Get extra card from Dad—he's got five.)

Mama Jardin—Day-Glo apron (Get material and ask Mom to help sew it!) $6.00

Granny Ryan—hand cream $6.00

Uncle Harvey—kazoo? harmonica? juggling balls? Slinky? $3.00

John Robert—windup toy $2.00
Blanca—friendship bracelet (find white and turquoise yarn) $3.00
Natalie—friendship bracelet (find black and purple yarn) $3.00
Katie—blank notebook for a journal $3.00
Charlie and Lily Alexander—spinning tops $4.00 ($2.00 each)
Mrs. Dudley—holly wreath and candle (ask Mom to help make)
Mrs. Howard—holly wreath and candle (ask Mom to help make)
Finish making picture frames for all the Ryans and Jardins.
TOTAL: $65.50, plus postage.
No way!

Today was our last day of school till next year. Before the bell rang for homeroom, I got to talk to Miss Dupré for a few minutes. I gave her my present—I got her a pen-and-ink set—and she gave me a hug. Then I said, "Miss Dupré, do you have 150 braids?" She winked at me and pretended to zip up her lips. She must be 30!

Monday, December 22

I got this letter today from Chloë Allen—all the way from
Louisiana:

Dear Ms. Fiona Claire Jardin,

> *You don't know me. My name is Chloë LaRue
> Allen. I am 13 years old, and I live in New Orleans,
> Louisiana. My dad's best friend is your teacher, Miss
> Jasmine Evangeline Teresa Jefferson Dupré.*
> *Jasmine Dupré is my good friend, too. And she's a
> friend of my mom's. I believe you know that Miss
> Dupré sent me a copy of your journal. I guess she
> thought it would make me feel better, because my
> parents are getting divorced and everything. I hope
> you won't be mad if I tell you that I threw your
> journal in the garbage. (No offense, but I don't like to
> even think about what's going to happen.) My dad
> took the journal out of the trash and asked me to put
> it in my desk drawer—in case I decided to read it
> after all.*
> *Sometimes I have a hard time falling to sleep at
> night. One night last week I started to read your
> journal. I read the whole thing straight through.
> Thank you for letting Jasmine Dupré copy it for me. I
> do NOT want my mom and dad to get divorced, but it*

sounds like your life is sort of OK even though your parents aren't together anymore.

You are a good writer. I hope everything is working out for you and Sam and Blanca and Katie and Natalie and Dylan and Jamil and everybody.

Sincerely,

Chloë LaRue Allen

P.S. Sam sounds like an angel compared to my little sister. Her name is Madeline. She's 8 years old, and she is a major brat.
P.P.S. If you write me a letter back, we could be pen pals.

Jasmine Dupré! That's what Chloë Allen calls Miss Dupré. Chloë sounds nice. I've never had a pen pal—except for Uncle Harvey. How strange to know that a girl like me read my journal in Louisiana. At least she liked it—and she's a teenager! I don't know much about Chloë LaRue Allen. Maybe tomorrow I'll write her a letter.

Madeline is a good name—and it doesn't have a fancy accent or an umlaut!

Tuesday, December 23

I wrote a long letter to Chloë Allen in New Orleans.

Right off I told her I'm glad she liked my journal—and I'm

not mad that she threw it in the garbage at first. I probably would have done the same thing if some kid I didn't know sent me pages and pages of stuff to read. But I bet it helped that Miss Dupré wrote Chloë a letter about me to go with my journal.

I don't mean to get into Chloë's business, but maybe things will work out OK for her family. Miss Dupré says that her mom and dad are exceptional—and so are Chloë and her little sister, Madeline. If Miss Dupré says they're all exceptional, they must be.

Just think. Miss Dupré must be back in New Orleans by now for Christmas. She's been sort of homesick, but I bet she'll be feeling fine once she has some gumbo and goes over to Plaisance to hear some zydeco music. Delaware is a long way from Louisiana. Maybe someday Chloë could come up here to visit— or I could go down there to check out the bayou.

Chloë is my first pen pal. I told her that Sam and Blanca and Natalie are fine—and that I don't see Katie and Dylan so much anymore. I also told her that most of the time Jamil is too shy to talk to me! And I sent her a friendship bracelet I made from yarn left over from Blanca's and Natalie's bracelets.

I hope Chloë likes turquoise and purple. I also hope she has a good Christmas—even though her parents are getting divorced.

It's snowing, snowing, snowing.

Two trees. Two stockings. One crèche—at Dad's. One ginger-bread house—at Mom's. And presents at both houses!

Dad's on vacation the rest of the week. He's taking us to church in a little while with Mama and Papa Jardin and Uncle Harvey. I hope the pageant isn't a dud. I'm one of the Wise Men, the one with frankincense. (Sam calls them the Wise Guys. He's the Star in the East.) Katie is the Virgin Mary. She's really embarrassed, but it could be worse—Dylan's a donkey. A bunch of my Jardin aunts and uncles and cousins are coming tomorrow. They're all staying at the Country Inn because Dad's townhouse is so small.

After church me and Sam are going over to Mom's for oyster stew (Yuck!) with 14 Ryans from all over the place. Dad and Mama and Papa and Uncle Harvey are coming, too. Dad loves Mom's oyster stew, but he said he can't stay too long. I bet he has to give Sarah her present.

What a crazy mixed-up Christmas. But Sam and I got to plan the whole thing with Mom and Dad. This way Sam and I get to see everybody. I wish we all still lived in the house on Orchard Lane. Sam barely even remembers our old house, but I do. When I was very young, four or five years ago, every time we pulled into the driveway at that house, my mom and dad would say that nursery rhyme: "Home again, home again. Jiggity-jig." Mom still says it every time we get home. So does Dad when we drive up to his townhouse, except he says: "Home again, home again. Jiggity-jog." Pig, hog. Jig, jog. It's pretty much the same.

It sounds silly, but I like it when I hear my mom and dad say that nursery rhyme. Then I know I'm home—wherever I am.

Thursday, December 25

This is the most incredible Christmas!

It didn't start out so great. The very first thing, Sam ran away. When I woke up, he was gone. Granny Ryan and Aunt Shaun started squawking right off. Granny wanted to call the police, but Mom said not to panic.

Sometimes Sam's not all that smart for a 6-year-old. He rode off on the two-wheeler Santa brought him (Right!), so me and Mom just followed his tire tracks through the snow. He pedaled straight down to the pond. When we got there, we found his new bike but no Sam. Mom freaked. Sam must have heard her calling him because then he started to yell like crazy.

We found him in some mulberry bushes. And there were my old roller skates! My binoculars and tambourine. Mom's paint-brushes and Sam's baseball mitt. Dad's harmonica. My Amherst College sweatshirt and Mom's left tennis shoe. My camera and sunglasses. There were heaps of tin foil, ice-cream sandwich wrappers, and bunches of Lucky Charms boxes. Plus, Sam's slingshot and my rhinestone barrettes. Every bit of our missing stuff.

There was a space cleared out under the bushes, and it

looked like a circus in there. Sam was curled up like a little quahog, clutching his slingshot and crying. He said he had thrown my roller skates in there a long time ago because I had snitched to Mom that he was throwing dirt clods at me and Blanca.

Then he got this idea: He was so mad at Mom and Dad about the divorce, he started throwing other stuff in there, too. He figured that if everybody's best stuff kept disappearing, Mom and Dad and me and him would have to work together to find it. Sam thought that if we were all on the same team, Snippers would come home. And Mom and Dad would stop being divorced.

Sam even hid some of his own stuff so that no one would get too suspicious. Mom got very quiet, and Sam cried harder and harder. It was like someone turned the hose on full blast. (I know what <u>that</u> feels like.) Mom hugged him and told him to slow down and breathe. When Sam finally stopped crying, he asked how long he'd have to be in Time-Out. Mom said they'd talk about that later.

Sam turned all red and <u>glub-glub-glubbed</u> some more. He finally looked up at Mom and said: "Snippers isn't coming back, is she?" Mom was quiet for a minute. Then she looked right into Sam's eyes and said, "No, Sugar Bear, Snippers is gone." She took a deep breath. "Sam, Dad and I aren't getting back together, either."

I guess I knew that, but I didn't really believe it until Mom said it out loud. I felt all heavy and sad for a minute, but then something in me fluttered and felt lighter. Sam didn't talk for a long time, but then he said, "So, can we make some snow angels before I have to go to Time-Out?"

And we did—big ones in the clearing behind the pond. It was so quiet and cozy.

I'm not sure what happened by the pond. Maybe it was magic. Or maybe it was just being happy about Christmas and finding Sam. But there I was, lying in the snow, flapping my arms and looking up at the fluffy clouds in the sky. It felt like I was flying. I started to laugh, and I couldn't stop! Mom and Sam were flapping in the snow, too. Soon all three of us were laughing. The wind whistled through the trees and the snow swirled all around us. Just like in my Lake Placid snow globe. I was wishing that somehow that very minute—me and Sam and Mom making snow angels—could be put in a snow globe forever. Then I could go back to that time and place whenever I want to. I wished Dad could have been there, too.

After a while we packed up all the stuff. Sam's nose was runny and I was frozen. We came home to Mom's, made cocoa, and opened more presents. Those Ryans are a noisy bunch! Mom is baking sticky buns and soda bread. It smells like cinnamon and hot chocolate and yeast and blue spruce in here. All Christmasy and . . . happy. Just like I remember from always.

Mom did a painting for me and Sam. It's the first one she's finished since she and Dad split up. It's got flying sneakers and talking teakettles all over it. Really wild—way better than Dylan's enchanted forest. And I got a portable CD player! Plus headphones and three CDs: Bach's <u>Goldberg Variations,</u> Celtic folk songs, and Jewel. The CD player had a note attached: "Miss Fiona Claire Jardin, Wise Guys are never too old to believe. S. Claus."

S. Claus? Right!

I have to go now. I can hear Dad out front, honking and laughing. We're all going skating down on the pond before Sam and I go over to Dad's. I can't wait to see his face when he sees the mug I made him. It says MUGwump on it. Mom helped me fire it extra hard in her friend Elle's kiln. We glazed it so that it's real shiny and bright.

Merry, merry Christmas!

Sunday, December 28

I flipped through my whole journal this morning.

I'm a little sad to see this year end. It's weird to think that more than a year has gone by since my mom and dad were still married—almost two years since we were all together on Orchard Lane. It's strange, too, to think that going back and forth between Mom's house and Dad's townhouse feels almost normal.

On March 4, I wrote: "Nothing is going to change. Ever." But lots of stuff has changed this year. A year ago I couldn't do decimals, and I didn't know anything about lockers or how to go from classroom to classroom at middle school. I didn't know much about poetry, either. Plus, now my favorite color is turquoise instead of purple. And Natalie is my second-best friend. Mom and Dad are sort of friendly now. And I almost never get stomachaches, unless I overload on Reese's Pieces—they're Dad's favorite candy, too. (Mom likes red licorice Twizzlers.) Mom's painting again. She's having a gallery show in the spring, and she's taking classes at the university for a master's degree on nights when Sam and I are at Dad's. (She's studying to become a landscape architect, which is perfect—then Mom can draw <u>and</u> work on gardens.) Plus, she's awesome with a cordless screwdriver. Dad's gotten to be a really good cook, and he sews much better than Mom does. One of his stories has been nominated for a big award.

A year ago I thought <u>divorce</u> was always spelled with a capital <u>D</u>. Like the Declaration of Independence. <u>Divorce</u> isn't a proper noun, and you don't need to capitalize it unless it's the first word in a sentence.

I can't believe it, but a year ago I barely knew John Robert—and I hadn't even met Miss Dupré yet! I was wrong in March—it's hard to believe that was only nine months ago. Things <u>do</u> change, even when they seem so bad you think you'll never be happy again.

Monday, December 29

Uh-oh. Dad just called.

He said Sam has some explaining to do—Melville had babies again! Seven this time. I said maybe we could name the babies after the Seven Wonders of the World—like we could call one Babylon and one Zeus. Dad said maybe we should name them after the Seven Deadly Sins instead. Who would name a rat Gluttony?

Dad said either way, we have to find them new homes or take them to the pet shop.

Tuesday, December 30

John Robert asked if I could come see him today, because tomorrow is New Year's Eve and he's taking the day off.

I think he kind of fired me. I guess you don't really get fired when you talk with a therapist. But it doesn't seem like there's so much hard stuff for me and John Robert to talk about anymore. Maybe that's because I can figure out some things for myself—and the rest of it Mom and Dad and Blanca and Miss Dupré can help me with.

John Robert wouldn't say yes or no, but I'm pretty sure the thing he wanted me to know is that I can trust myself—but I'm not all alone. He said that sometimes divorce makes kids grow up too fast. He also said that I'm lucky for lots of reasons—especially because my parents understand that it's important for me and Sam to feel safe and happy just being kids. More than anything else, John Robert wanted to know what I, <u>Fiona Claire Jardin,</u> think about M-E.

When I told him my life is OK—and that I laughed so hard on Christmas Day because I was really happy—John Robert said that laughter is a great gift. He said laughter often means there's something tickling your heart. I like that idea a lot. (Maybe John Robert should be a poet instead of a therapist.) Then he said that he thought it was time for us to say good-bye. At least for now.

I cried just a little because I didn't know how to thank him. But I know John Robert understands. I asked him if we can still be friends. John Robert smiled and said, "Always." He gave me a little package wrapped in gold paper tied with purple ribbons. It feels like a book. Then he said, "It is a great honor to know you, Fiona Claire Jardin. My door will always be open if you would ever like to talk." We shook hands and I started to laugh. I don't know why, but I couldn't help it. It just seemed funny that John Robert was acting so professional.

At least he made a goofy face at me when he waved good-bye.

Wednesday, December 31

Good-bye to this year!

365 days. A whole year. It wasn't so bad. Actually, it was pretty good—way better than last year. Mom says next year will be even better. Maybe she's right.

Sam and I are at Dad's. He started making the black-eyed peas for tomorrow. We rented <u>Star Wars</u> and <u>The Terminator,</u> but Dad fell asleep on the couch. Sarah's bringing sparkling cider and pizza later. She's sort of nice, but not one bit like my mom. She gave me a great set of colored markers and sparkly purple nail polish for Christmas. And she painted my fingernails. (Sarah doesn't know that Mom lets me wear polish on my toenails but <u>not</u> on my fingernails. Mom thinks fingernail polish looks too grown-up for an 11½-year-old girl. I'd better remember to take the polish off before I go over to Mom's house on Sunday.)

Mom and Dad have some plan that we'll take turns with holidays every year. It makes me dizzy to even think about it, but we should be at Mom's for New Year's Eve when I'm 16. I figured it out. (Sometimes I'm glad I'm OK at math.) It will be a Monday night, and I'll be driving by then! Dad says that's scary, but I can't wait to drive.

Me and Sam and Dad went for a long walk this morning. Dad said that while we wait for the New Year to come tonight, we have to tell the best and the worst things about this year. I thought about that for a long time today.

There was plenty of bad stuff: Snippers never came home. We had to give Melville's babies back. (And now we will again.) I blew up big-time at Mom and Dad. But the worst thing is the same as last year: being divorced. Sometimes I worry that Dad and Sarah will get married, but Mom says worrying about stuff that <u>might</u> happen is a waste of time and energy.

It's harder to decide about the best thing. Blanca's still my best friend. I finally got Rollerblades. Halloween was the best ever, and Thanksgiving at the lake was pretty good, even though Mom wasn't there. My soccer team was undefeated.

And I met my first pen pal: Chloë LaRue Allen. Plus, I got my own room at both houses—and Mom and Dad each raised my allowance to $5 a week. Someday I might have enough money to go to Argentina with Blanca. Even keeping this journal turned out to be pretty good.

John Robert helped me a lot. And Miss Dupré is amazing, too. They sort of remind me of each other, even though he's a man and she's a woman. John Robert knows about lots of different things, and Miss Dupré teaches us such great stuff—like all about Greek mythology and gumbo! They are both excellent listeners.

But the best thing about this whole year is the same as last year, and the year before that, and since forever—my family. For the longest time, I worried that I'd forgotten how to laugh. But that wasn't what I'd forgotten at all. I'd forgotten that no matter what happens, I still have my family: Mom, Dad, and Sam—plus all the other Jardins and Ryans. I'd also forgotten that no matter what, I'm still me—the one and only Fiona Claire Jardin.

The year is done, and so is this journal. John Robert's present to me was a brand-new one. It's all clean and blank, except that I wrote *Fiona Claire Jardin* in my best cursive on the first page. It's a little scary and exciting to see an empty year open up in front of you.

I worked on my cinquain this afternoon. I think it might be done. I also started a sonnet. (Sonnets are tricky, because of the rules for rhyme scheme and meter.) It's about shoes, and the working title is "Sonnet in 6½B." So far all I have is the couplet for the ending. Miss Dupré says you can get trapped in a poem if you think you know where it's going to take you before you write it, but I can't help it—these lines flew into my head today:

> *In closets late at night shoes sing their song*
> *Of all the things they've seen and where they've gone.*

I wonder what's going to happen next. . . .

Home Again

Oak door
Swings wide. Warm light
Spills pools across cool planks.
Each step an old friend singing soft
Welcome.

ACKNOWLEDGMENTS

The list of people I am grateful to for making this short book possible is long.

For starters, my heartfelt thanks go to all the old friends in Denver, Colorado, who shared with my family the hopeful and sleep-deprived early years of marriage and parenthood. Thanks, too, to my newer but no less stalwart friends in San Diego, California, particularly the five intrepid women—Frankie Wright, Anne Marie Welsh, Maggie Locke, Dawn Diez Willis, and Marlane Miriello—who have come to know me not as half of a couple but as a singular mother and sometime writer.

I am also grateful to the retinue of professionals who helped us navigate the bumpy terrain of divorce: To James V. DeLeo and Eleanor Beitler-Kreyling for the psychological guidance they provided. To Dr. Andrew Israel for occasionally checking my pulse. To William Hargreaves and Mary Mudd-Quinn for shepherding my former husband and me through mediation. And to Bill Fuhrman, Esquire, for deciphering the mysteries of the law with expertise, grace, and welcome wit. My gratitude also extends to the teachers, students, and families at The Child's Primary School in San Diego, for opening their arms and their hearts to embrace my children when they most needed comfort. And most especially to Kari Katz (and David), our own beloved Mary Poppins.

This book would not have been possible without the fortitude of my colleagues at Harcourt Brace & Company—particularly my irrepressible editor, Allyn Johnston, who would not take no for an answer, and associate editor Susan Schneider, who laughed and cried when she first met Fiona. I am grateful to Michael Stearns, who extolled the arduous but satisfying work of revision. Thanks, too, to Lynn Harris, Kaelin Chappell, Lisa Peters, Pascha Gerlinger, and Erin DeWitt for turning a computer printout into this lovely book.

I could not have found my way through the swamp of sadness to Fiona and her family without the loving support of my own family. I am thankful for the sturdy peasant stock—the Irish grit and the Italian gusto—that is part of the legacy passed down from my father and my mother. I am indebted, too, to my sisters, Shauneen and Kathleen, for their steady kindness, and to my twin, John Robert, for his generous spirit and for walking with me every step of the way.

Most of all, I am grateful to my children: Andrew Stewart Bayer, Henry Eliot Bayer, and Hannah Caitlin Bayer. There's more than a little of each of them in this book, and not one of them would let me give up on nudging Fiona's journal into print. All three remind me daily—with their eager smiles and insatiable curiosity—that we share a grand adventure indeed . . . and that I am exquisitely blessed to be their mother.

Library of Congress Cataloging-in-Publication Data
Cruise, Robin, 1951–
The top-secret journal of Fiona Claire Jardin/Robin Cruise.
p.   cm.
Summary: At the suggestion of her therapist, ten-year-old Fiona begins to keep a journal
in which she records her fears, feelings, and gradual adjustment
in the year after her parents get a divorce.
ISBN 0-15-201383-0
[1. Divorce–Fiction.   2. Parent and child–Fiction.   3. Family life–Fiction.
4. Diaries–Fiction.]   I. Title.
PZ7.C88828To   1998
[Fic]–dc21   97-40363

Text set in Clearface
Display type hand-lettered by Robin Cruise
Designed by Kaelin Chappell

First edition

A   C   E   F   D   B

For Andrew, Henry, and Hannah
For Richard, their father—
And for families everywhere,
in all their shapes and sizes

Blessed are you that weep now, for you shall laugh.

Luke 6:21